The critics on Steve Ay

'Steve Aylett is without ambitious and talented new writers to emerge in England in recent years. While his work echoes the best of William Burroughs, it has the mark of real originality. It's hip, cool and eloquent. It's what Tom Wolfe would like to be. Aylett does effortlessly what others labour to achieve. He has a cold, accurate eye, a mocking wit and a black, playful angle of attack which has learned something from cyberpunk but has that smack of idiosyncrasy, that sense of exploring new territories, that laconic, confident humour which tells you that this is exactly the book you've been waiting for. Snap it up now. Before it snaps you'
Michael Moorcock

'Wickedly funny futuristic pulp thriller: James Ellroy meets Terry Pratchett in cyberspace. The crime novel of the future, or a virtual reality instruction manual? As far away from Agatha Christie as you can go' *Daily Telegraph*

'Comic-book imagery – like Jim Steranko on steroids – mingles with a noiriste's worst nightmare . . . Distressingly brilliant' *Guardian*

'Steve Aylett knows gumshoe future-slang like Irvine Welsh knows swearwords. Initially his fast, culturally referential style leaves you gasping for air . . . but dive in and you'll be dragged along . . . a terrific read, full of armoury-loving cops, dimension-travelling robbers and the pursuit of a precious totemic book. Like Dashiell Hammett scripting a story for *2000 AD* space-girl Halo Jones, this is sci-fi for non-geeks'
The Face

'Aylett's prose is like poetry' *Independent*

'Prodigiously paranoid routines delivered with a toxic fizz. A catalogue of synapse-scorching similes any bankrupt Martian poet would kill for. Watch them scatter like buckshot through the works of all self-respecting thieves and plagiarists' Iain Sinclair

'A dizzying psychedelic rush' *The Times*

'Writes like a man possessed by comic demons . . . the pages pop in your hands like firecrackers'
Evening Standard

Steve Aylett was born in 1967. He is the author of *Bigot Hall, Slaughtermatic* and *The Inflatable Volunteer* and was a Philip K. Dick Award nominee. If he were any more English he'd be dead.

THE CRIME STUDIO

STEVE AYLETT

INDIGO

An Indigo paperback
First published in Great Britain by Serif in 1994
This paperback edition published in 2000 by Indigo,
an imprint of Orion Books Ltd,
Orion House, 5 Upper St Martin's Lane, London WC2H 9EA

A CIP catalogue record for this book is available from the British Library.

ISBN 0 575 40294 6

Printed in Great Britain by
The Guernsey Press Co. Ltd, Guernsey, Channel Islands

'How come I know so much? What the hell is going on around here? Who the hell *are* you people?'

Roy Neary,
Close Encounters of the Third Kind

Contents

SOLITARY

Joe Solitary was a baby-faced guy with a sublime introversion and a deep self-destructive streak which endeared him to the denizens of Beerlight. Solitary got his name from a love of solitary confinement, which he said really got him *into* himself.

But this was not the first and by no means the most deep-seated of his obsessions. When he was at school Solitary had been chastised for a misbehaviour he did not commit, and while most of us would conclude from this that there is nothing to be gained from obeying the rules, Sol was more impressionable — he loved the martyr-like buzz of false accusation and in later life used every trick in the book to be arrested and imprisoned for crimes in which he had played no part whatsoever. Being black helped. Sol scanned the papers for whatever crimes had been accomplished lately and dropped by the cop den to confess.

At first he was smiling and reckless, claiming

responsibility for armed robberies, auto thefts, political hostage-taking and even boxing fatalities in regard to which thousands of spectators could and would attest his innocence. The multiplicity of his allegations and his breathtaking lack of motive made the cops suspicious — even Chief of the Cops Henry Blince, who was the kind of cop a kid would draw.

Sol soon realised he'd blown the gaff. Everyone knew he was crazy and that he wanted to be sent down for no good reason. The clincher came when he claimed to be the ringleader of a gang which had achieved a spectacular bullion raid and the real ringleader came forward and indignantly proclaimed his own guilt, presenting photographs to prove it.

Sol was a laughing stock. He didn't even know the true facts of the crimes he'd put himself up for. He was a failure as a wrongful conviction.

Solitary decided to try a different approach. He knew he needed to lay out the scam to the cops before the story hit the headlines — maybe even before the crime had been reported. So he attempted to infiltrate the underworld and get the grapevine on whatever improving affairs were brewing up. He tried to get chummy with the real crooks, but when they saw him approaching — sad-eyed — they'd huddle and swear, telling him to take his innocence and shove it. Everybody knew that Sol was getting desperate.

It was inevitable that at some time an antidude would have the brains to recognise Solitary's value as an alibi. This person was Billy Panacea, burglar extraordinaire, known to the denizens of Beerlight as a man who could think without moving his legs. Billy's life of crime had begun in his late teens when he broke a bottle over a guy's head and was arrested for impersonating a cop. From that day he was always on the lookout for a scam which would fool the constabulary because he knew what alot of crooks didn't — that the most important part of any crime is to get away with it.

Billy Panacea approached Sol with a proposition. Sol would join Billy and the gang on a flying visit to a premises one evening — Billy and the gang would spin-dry the safe and Sol would sit and think about the Holy Trinity. He wouldn't even have to carry anything. It would be Sol's responsibility to slam his prints on the safe, the window and a crowbar which they'd leave behind. Then the next morning he'd go to the cops, confess everything and implicate Billy and the gang. The cops would dismiss the whole thing as a sophisticated attempt by Sol to get sent to the state pen and Billy and the gang would be cleared along with him — if Sol said they were there, nobody would believe they were within a million miles of the place. Sol wouldn't get any time, but to compensate Billy would give him a share of the proceeds. It was a daring plan, but as Billy knew and as Billy's attorney would repeatedly proclaim, 'The law is where reality goes to die.'

The raid started out like a dream. Billy's gang at this time consisted of the cracker twins Brailleface and Hangerhead. They were so easy with the dial they spent the early part of the break-in sniggering fiercely at Sol, who didn't mind a bit. He watched from an armchair, a beatific smile splitting his features as the door swung. Billy stood at the window on the lookout, now and again turning to the twins and snapping commands like a harassed sniper. Sol pawed the premises, plastering his fingerprints over anything sturdy enough to hold them. By the end of his rounds he was looking tireder than Al Pacino and slumped into the armchair again.

'Unless I am sadly mistaken this is no time for a rest,' shouted Billy Panacea.

'Don't worry about me,' said Sol. 'I'll be alright in a minute.' But he was clearly nodding off.

This calibre of exhaustion in such a huge guy was a cause for concern among Billy and the gang, and they began to fear that they'd be collared by a friendly neighbour or patrolling cop. 'Let's get out of here Joe, or we'll be in the soup until the rattle in our dying throats relieves us.'

But Sol was asleep. Sol was *snoring*. Billy and the gang grabbed ahold and tried to lift him out of it but Sol was as heavy and loud as a whale that had swallowed a foghorn and Billy was getting nervous. Sol was snoring loud enough to wake up Billy's dead grandmother and right now that was the last person to whom Billy wanted to explain himself. Every attempt at waking Sol was met with cowlike inertia.

'It aint no use,' whined Billy, 'we'll have to leave him and hope he stays dumb.' Billy Panacea and the gang cleared out leaving Sol sound asleep in a corner.

The cops had a field day. There was more evidence

than they could comprehend, and god knows he had a motive. 'So you finally did it, eh Joe?' said Chief Henry Blince.

'That's right Chief,' said Solitary, beaming. 'I did it alright. My prints are all over this premises.'

Sol was sentenced to twenty years, and he sat in his cell chuckling at what could be achieved with a well-measured dose of sleeping tablets.

Two weeks later Billy Panacea and the gang brought Sol's contentment to an end when, in a fit of remorse and criminal fraternity, they nitroed the jail and busted him out.

GUILT COMPLEX

Brute Parker ran the all-night gun shop on the corner of Dive and Ride, and it was a valuable service he offered. Anyone needing a gun fast at three in the morning ran round to Parker's store to view the extensive range. But nobody ever haggled with Brute Parker, whose philosophy was, 'Well whatever it was, it's dead now.' He had a polaroid in his pocket of a moment when he was calm.

There was only one guy in Beerlight meaner than Brute Parker — a guy called Auto-Rhino — and he was in maximum security for cannibalising his fellow passengers in an elevator when it stopped between floors for five minutes. With Auto-Rhino out of the picture, Parker was the biggest professional shithead in town.

Now it was amazing to the denizens of Beerlight that Aggie Swan the head should have any dealings with Brute Parker. Aggie Swan was a toxic beauty who had perfected the 'wasted angel' look to such a pitch that people shielded their eyes against the expected atomic blast of her ascension. Chemically she was more than human. Her eyes were all the colours of the spangled banner. Her hair wasn't just blond, it was transparent. It was a right hook to the glass jaw of the underworld when she and Parker stepped out as a couple. Beauty and the beast — when they approached, nobody knew whether to laugh or cry. Someone might have dared ask Aggie what drew her to Parker, but in the presence of Aggie's loving eyes anyone with a guilty secret would become ashamed, with the result that almost nobody in Beerlight ever spoke to her. Meanwhile in defiance of all the principles of a learning relationship, Aggie and Brute caused a scary ballooning of one-another's characteristics – Aggie grew more and more angelic, while Brute no longer bothered even to look at who he was knifing.

It came about that Brute got in the soup with the city council and, putting on a suit, addressed Aggie like this: 'My rent is under intense review and I must go before the panel of this fair city and defend myself due to the charges of disturbance of the peace surrounding my boutique, what with the clientele testing the merchandise in the small hours. I have tied a string to my finger so as to remember not to mention the ten simultaneous people I shot all at once in the Delayed Reaction Bar last year. You must take care of the boutique while I'm off, seeing as my regular front man Lou is not available due to a friend having unfortunately strapped him to the front of a locomotive just when he was least expecting it.'

So as Aggie minded the store and day moved into night the first customer arrived — Billy Panacea, burglar extraordinaire, who dashed into the shop in a black outfit having just fallen through the skylight of a townhouse on Chain Street and landed amid the silverware of an elegant supper attended by the Chief of the Cops and the Mayor's wife. Now the cops were on him and he needed a knife at least. But confronted by the smiling and innocent expectancy on the face of Aggie Swan, he found himself as meek as a lamb, unable to shriek his predicament and, bowing his head, asked for a refill for his lighter. He was in an alley clutching the lighter and sobbing when the cops arrested him for dressing in black and scaring the Chief. Customer number one.

The second customer was Sammy Vale, who ran out of the night in fear of death at the hands of Kicker Charlie to whom he owed a thousand smackers in gambling regret. But seeing Aggie's calm, eager-to-please tilt of the head, Vale turned pale. Ignoring the revolvers, he sheepishly took a handful of lemondrops from a tub by the ammunition cupboard, doled out five smackers he could ill afford and backed out. The next day he was in a wheelchair. Customer number two.

It was three in the morning when in came a guy whose face resembled something glimpsed through the porthole of a bathysphere. This gentleman was none other than Auto-Rhino, who had just incidentally busted out of maximum security and was now under obligation to shoot the life out of anyone who came near him. He was all fired up to tear Brute Parker's head off and select firearms at his leisure but he was totally thrown at the sight of Aggie Swan, who looked up from a copy of *Mondo* and regarded him with eyes that wouldn't quit. There was something about her that made him want to pour out his heart, or at the very least someone else's. But Auto-Rhino could only speak in words of less than one syllable. How could he explain to her that it was due to his mother's neglect that he had eaten those eight people in the elevator? He was mortified that a woman like this should see him wearing these tasteless widestripe pyjamas.

At twenty-five black minutes past four in the morning Brute Parker returned hale and hearty to the gun shop. He'd remembered not to mention his participation in the Delayed Reaction Bar Massacre with a suavity he had not known he possessed, and with everything on the up and up he had caroused until this very hour. Pinned to the army surplus tub was a note which read like this: 'Darling Parker — I have gone with Auto-Rhino where no one will ever care to find us. Do not think badly of me. There is no good without bad, and I have always needed a bastard to balance the energy in the relationship deal. It is for this reason that I came to Beerlight. It sure beats going to Tibet. Seeing as Auto is badder than you, what with him eating all those unfortunate people, maybe this time I will attain total enlightenment. Be well. Aggie.'

Well Parker was out of sorts for days, and once neglected to shoot someone who had it coming. At one point I myself thought I saw Parker looking at the pattern on a fallen leaf, though I wouldn't swear to it. The denizens of Beerlight were worried for him, but within a fortnight he was back on form and had even returned to paying proper attention to who he was knifing. I figured it was the passage of time but it turned out Parker was chuffed — Auto had walked back to stir with his own legs, leaving Aggie high and dry. 'Whenever I was gonna flatten some guy,' Auto whispered to the warden, 'she would look at me, and I found I didn't have the heart. Then she would give me the back for being soft. It was a circle of vicious shape, warden, and I tell you one thing — the sooner I am locked up the more harm I will feel free to do.'

EXTERMINATOR

I bumped into Tony Endless at the Delayed Reaction Bar on Valentine Street — he was sat in a booth drinking a shake that was built so badly all the drugs had risen to the surface. Tony was looking more depressed than someone due to attend the opera and I was grotesquely surprised, as in all the years I'd known him Tony Endless had been the happiest man in the nation. He once tried scream therapy and found he could only whistle. Seeing him in a gloom at the Reaction I feared the worst.

'Tony Endless, you bastard in a million,' I enquired gently, 'what is the cause of this grim exterior?'

'My exterior is all it should be,' Tony Endless replied, 'considering what I have just experienced.'

'I will order three more shakes,' I told him. 'Relate to me in finely-crafted detail what is bothering you.'

'Well,' said Tony Endless, and described the following events. 'I had landed the righteous job of pest controller, that is, a character who exterminates unwanted creature infestations in the houses of the denizens of Beerlight. Now I'll have you know as well as I do that it is difficult enough for me to keep a job due to my general inability to look fearful and depressed in the workplace. And so I was determined to keep this post. This very morning I visited my first customers, a happy-looking couple in a big house out on Chain Street. Well no sooner had I entered the premises than I discovered a dog right there in the living room — naturally I dispatched it right off. The occupants let out a yell, and I explained to them that the report they had heard was just a cough from my handgun. I proceeded immediately to the kitchen, where after a cursory examination I detected a housecat sitting real quiet on the window ledge, so I gave it a quick burst from the old Thompson my daddy gave me — the one Brute Parker wanted to buy? — took it out with one squeeze. There was a glass water tank in the bedroom, and I tell you it was *swarming* with every kind of fish with a name. What an eye-opener — this place was infested. I got out my sledgehammer — the big one? — and bust in the front of the tank. The occupants came in and screamed, seeing the water and weeds on the floor, but that's the price you pay for hygiene, right?

'So next I go up onto the roofgarden — real nice roofgarden — and almost straight away I perceive this big ugly goddamn *tortoise* lumbering around, draggin' a piece of lettuce. Well by now I know how the gun startles people and I don't want to scare the whole neighbourhood, so I put on an oven mitt, pick this tortoise up and throw it over the edge. Right about then the occupants come out on to the roof, see — the wife's crying, out of gratitude I thought, and carrying that damned dog in both arms like damp laundry. 'Don't think nothin' of it lady,' I say. 'I'm just in it for the cash.'

'Well the guy of the house proceeds in the activity of rolling up his sleeves and advancing toward me, inexplicably bent on destruction. And since I am now lying on the garden chair in the knowledge of a job well done, I do not have my equipment right to hand and I am caught unawares. Now it is a practice of mine never to punch a man whose face is redder on the outside than mine is on the inside, and so I leapt up and ran as fast as my arms and legs could carry me. When I got to the office and told my employer of these incidents he nearly punched me with his knife and told me right out to never darken his life again. It seems that bad luck will cling to me like a dry fern for the whole of my formless career.'

Well after Tony Endless had finished relating all this to me, I advised him to go home and forget that these fashionable events had ever happened. After all, he wasn't the first guy to have shot a dog, especially in Beerlight. Tony agreed without enthusiasm and left the bar under a cloud of dejection. Framed momentarily in the doorway, he was like a window-perched saxman who had forgotten how to play.

It was four minutes past one the next afternoon

when Tony Endless re-entered the Delayed Reaction with a new exuberance.

'You know my unfortunate social gaffe yesterday morning?' he said to me, sitting down. 'The news of it has swept this town like a pestilence and been the catalyst for a most unexpected business opportunity. When I got home yesterday after conversing with you, the phone did not stop ringing. It seems there is a great demand for the absence of dogs and the like in certain homes, and here is the man who can provide that absence.'

I was as shocked as I was able.

'Do you mean to tell me you fully intend to stalk the Beerlight community shooting the life out of housedogs like some low-grade Travis Bickle?'

'No indeed,' he laughed. 'For I have discovered that there is a corresponding demand for the warm presence of such creatures in yet other homes. I can provide both services and be paid twice over. All I need is an answerphone, a landing net, a dogbasket, a flashlight and housebreaking lessons from someone such as Billy Panacea, burglar extraordinaire, and I'll be laughing fit to burst.'

And so it was. If anyone wanted to be rid of such mammals and reptiles as they possessed without the authorities or others in the household knowing of this desire, that person would call the Tony Endless Bestial Relocation Service — and under cover of darkness Tony would convey these creatures to those who had contacted him with a wish to care for them. Tony was his own boss. Within a year he had made a fortune, and he nocturnally replaced the pets of the couple on Chain Street — in fact they found such a frenzied menagerie of stepping and winged animals in their home I bet they're too busy to remember Tony Endless, or even to go out and make a decent living.

HIT

There's nothing so degrading as being killed by a stranger. It wrecks continuity. Murder should occur among friends, or so went the opinion of Brute Parker who ran the all-night gun shop on the corner of Dive and Ride. So when Terry Tremelo asked him a certain favour, Brute was uncooperative. The target was a total stranger living in Maui, and despite Terry Tremelo's mafia connections Parker was bound to refuse.

'Parker,' said Terry Tremelo, 'I'll have you know as well as I do this aint a mob hit — this guy double-crossed me in a bit of business I was working on the side and I want him in lavender at the nearest and dearest opportunity. Do you mean to stand by these unholy principles?'

'As I would stand by a friend's grave, Terry Tremelo — I do not know the guy and if I were to ventilate him, my associates would think me reckless and uncouth. And anyway he is in Maui, and I do not care to see so many smiling faces.'

'Well here's an idea — ' said Tremelo, ' — go on over and get to know the guy — tell him you're on vacation. Then when you're good pals, air him out. Anyone smiles at you, bust 'em in the nose same as you do here. But listen, my bet is you'll wanna bury the guy soon as you meet him — even his brain's got a tan.'

Now Brute could not see any argument against this, especially with Terry offering twenty thousand smackers up front, so he left El Henry in charge of the store and headed out. He took a modified Remington automatic which he took apart and mailed ahead in gift wrapping, carrying only the barrel onto the plane disguised as an extra broad stick of macaroni.

The target's name was Luke Amble — Brute located him at a bar and was about to start a conversation when Luke ordered a round for everyone and began letting off firecrackers. Then everyone went down to the beach and proceeded in the activity of eating coconuts and Luke Amble, laughing fit to burst, opened ten crates of beer. Luke Amble balanced a barbecue spike on his nose while doing the limbo, then took a load of people out to teach them to waterski. Now it was a great surprise to Brute Parker to find himself among the people being taught this skill, and an even greater surprise to find he was getting a blast out of it. Looking down he found he was wearing shorts and a Hawaiian shirt. He could ski-jump better than anyone off the ramps. In fact

Brute was in his element among these characters, and a figure of great popularity. Over the next three days he and Luke were inseparable and at one point set fire to the pants of a priest, staggering off in a rictus of hilarity. Luke Amble was a nice guy who was generous to everyone.

One day the two were sipping tequilas at the beach bar and Brute Parker addressed Luke Amble like this: 'I have certainly enjoyed this visit to Maui, Luke Amble. You have taught me to ski on the water and I had always believed that the only use for such a fluid was in the flushing away of my throat-knife on the arrival of the cops. Why I can even view the scenery in sunlight without wanting to barf. Luke Amble, you are a friend of mine if ever there was one. But Luke, I have a fiery confession. Terry Tremelo has paid me twenty thousand smackers to shoot you in the face until dead.'

Now at this Luke Amble poured his tequila into the wrong orifice he was so surprised, and began begging for mercy, weeping in the shade of the pineapples. And he soon began to yammer about Terry's bit of business on the side and how Terry was laundering the mob's money until it was practically his own, and how Luke had ceased to help him on realising to whom the money rightly belonged. For this Terry wanted Luke aired out, and to top it all Luke described Terry as such a shyster as to be almost from Texas.

'Well Luke,' stated Brute Parker, 'do not trouble yourself on account of my bloody mission. I find that you have done so much for me that I am a changed man — in fact I may have changed by as much as eight percent, and that's good enough for me. I promise that your face and body will remain intact, as a carefree gesture of my esteem.'

Luke Amble was most relieved at this turn of events, not to mention in clinical shock — but Parker was nagged by a detail. 'My old friend Terry Tremelo has paid me to do a job,' he said, 'and I'll have you know as well as I do my Remington is expecting to be let out for some exercise.'

Well it happened that the mob didn't mind when Terry Tremelo was found drilled full of beans from a Remington automatic as they had it from Brute Parker he'd been doing a little business on the side. And if there's one thing the mob deplore, it's an abuse of friendship.

SENTIMENT

Billy Panacea, burglar extraordinaire, was regarded by the denizens of Beerlight as a young man of enterprise. There were few souls below the age of thirty who would choose such a traditional, specialised and thankless profession, especially without a gun. And because he looked so benign Billy got away with alot early on — the first time he was arrested with an overnight bag of burgled goods he was fined for opening a door with an expired loyalty card.

It was Billy's belief that there are some things that don't exist in retail reality — they exist in the reality of stealing or being stolen. All it takes is a little personality. For him, cracking wasn't a challenge but a physical form of sarcasm. He told me that doors were invented to let people in and out, and that as long as doors were included in the design of safes, vaults and houses, they would continue to serve this purpose.

However, there was one safe Billy had never been

able to penetrate. This safe had originally been acquired by Dane Eliot, an old hand who it seemed had bungled the job and carried the safe away in the hope of blowing it later. Dane was as savage as a dog and had gotten so angry during the course of the burglary that he killed his partner, severing the guy's head and leaving a mess on the premises. Billy Panacea intercepted the safe just after Dane's arrest and it was now his habit to tinker with it between crimes, trying out a new gizmo or explosive on each occasion. Billy did not want the box on display at his place in case he should have critical visitors and so I myself agreed to keep it in my yard.

Billy told me the safe was made of high-security armour. He tried using a core drill, which caved in the side-wall and made Billy nervous; a torch, which did nothing; and even some old-fashioned slow-burn acid. Finally he hit it with an 84mm round from an AT8 anti-tank gun while I was eating breakfast. I ran out to the yard in great alarm to find Billy crouching in front of the blasted-open safe. Clearly visible in the safe was a guy's head which was sadly not accompanied by a body.

'Billy you twisted son of a bitch,' I yelled, 'how dare you secrete a severed head in my yard, even if it is surrounded by high-security armour. Get it out of here on the double or I'll be sick.'

'This safe was hermetically sealed — ' Billy marvelled, ' — the head is in tip-top condition and has not decomposed in the slightest.'

'What does it matter the condition of the head,' I

shouted. 'You cannot have a severed head unclaimed in Beerlight.'

'This head is not unclaimed,' laughed Billy. 'This is the head of Dane Eliot's partner in crime, whom Dane decapitated the night the safe was removed from the premises. It is a fact of the matter that nobody ever found this item and that nobody could identify the corpse without it. Dane is gonna love us.'

Well I had my doubts about this notion but Billy Panacea insisted we slam the head in the refrigerator and pay a visit to Dane in the state pen. Dane was pleased to see us until we mentioned the item in the safe, at which he took a drag on the wrong end of his cigarette and commenced in the activity of sneering through the grill of the visitors' barrier. 'Billy,' he said to Billy, 'I have been concerned about the location of that safe since the cops picked me up — I should have known a young gun like you would acquire it. Armour-piercing shells eh Billy? You could not use that on a premises in the dark hours.'

'How did you open the safe that night, Dane?' Billy asked him. 'And why did you use it to stash the bonce?'

'I will not tell you how I opened that box,' laughed Dane, 'for in six years I will get out of here and you and I will be in competition. But I wound down my partner that evening because he had given me info on the contents of the safe — cash and other trinkets beyond our imagining he said. And when I opened it, there were no contents whatever. I became emotional and my partner's head got a little loose — so I stashed it in the safe and drove it to the basement on Hole Street. And here I am doing only ten years. It is lucky Captain Orlok retired from the force just before then or I would be doing twenty.'

'Did this Captain Orlok have a downer on you?' I asked.

'No indeed,' said Dane in a mysterious manner. 'Some people is stupid, is all.'

'Some people might say you are not a bulging genius for being here in the state pen,' remarked Billy Panacea, and Dane became indignant.

'I have more brains than you, Billy Panacea, so-called burglar extraordinaire, who cannot open a box without the aid of a howitzer. I have outsmarted the cops because I am right in one unholy respect — they could not identify the body without the head. There is no end of denizens of Beerlight with Chairman Mao tattooed on their chest.' Dane laughed. 'Anyhow, the item you found is surely rotted beyond recognition by now.'

'On the contrary,' announced Billy Panacea, 'it is as fresh as a babe and I recognise the face upon it as though it were yesterday. In fact I intend to name names to the authorities in two shakes of a lamb's tail.'

At this Dane spat out his gasper and began to cough like a theatregoer, looking fearfully aside at the prison guards. 'Keep your relentless voice down Billy Panacea.'

'I will if you tell me how you opened that box so quiet,' said Billy.

Dane thought about it. 'You have me over a barrel

and through a glass darkly, Billy Panacea. Gimme a pen and tell that clown to look the other way.'

Well I was aggrieved at being referred to as a clown, and in consequence decided to peek at what Dane was writing down. But he wasn't writing anything down — he was breaking off the end of the pen in a particular manner and handing it back to Billy. 'This will take you into any safe in the country before you can say Saint Peter. Now get out of here Billy and keep your shapeless mouth shut.'

That very night Billy paid a nocturnal visit to a premises he'd had his eye on, and the customised pen worked like a fish. When Billy came by the next morning to dispose of the head he was as happy as a dog in a sidecar. As we weighted the item and dropped it into the bay I asked Billy to whom it rightly belonged.

'It is the noggin of none other than Captain Orlok,' laughed Billy. 'That safe resided at the cop den, and Captain Orlok must have told Dane what it contained the day he left the force. The contents were in fact the various articles I myself acquired at the age of twenty on my very first nocturnal job, and which were found on my person by Captain Orlok himself. This is why the box has such sentimental value. The goods must have been returned to their original owner before Dane got there — but finding Captain Orlok himself in the box is worth all my efforts. I remember he stood up for my character in court. I would recognise that dumb expression anywhere.'

TURNAROUND

It was more than trouble Tudor Garris got into when he emptied Kicker Charlie's casino on Valentine Street. If you win more than once at paynose you're either cheating or lucky, and both of these conditions are frowned upon by the management. In fact the management frown all the way to their fists, and any big win is signified by the sound of skulls breaking like crockery. It was while idly watching one lucky player plunge through the trashcans behind Kicker's casino that an idea kissed the mind of Tudor Garris. Just because you're a fool doesn't mean you're a loser.

There was a saying at Kicker's paynose table — 'Round and round and round it goes, and where it stops, only Kicker knows.' There was more machinery in Kicker's paynose table than in the history of the US space programme. With every spin of the wheel the national grid experienced a power drain. Depressives flocked to the table in the hope of catching a buzz. Serious players wore grounding boots. On one occasion the wheel wouldn't move because Kicker had forgotten to plug it in. Innovative bookies such as Lou Shallow took odds on whether players would die from cranial fractures or electrocution. The source-adjustable industrial magnet housed under the wheel was so powerful that bridgework, belts, daggers and handguns were yanked from the convulsing players and later sold back to them at prices which could only be seen in their entirety by means of a compound eye.

It was desolately clear to everyone that Kicker was the key, since he decided the winning digit. Some bet on Kicker's house number. For two months Tudor Garris went only 10 and 23, working a system based on the birthday of Kicker's mother. The gambler Sammy Vale, who owed Kicker a thousand smackers, rigged Kicker's house with subliminal speakers which repeated the number 25 over and over, but rather than induce Kicker to punch this number on the wheel, this elaborate system induced Kicker to punch Sammy Vale 25 times on the nose. Some said the spin never landed on 36 because Kicker couldn't count that far.

Tudor Garris finally paid a visit to his pal Ben Rictus at the power plant. The power company paid Ben barely enough to keep him in codeine, and Ben had a mordantly expensive project to pursue. Garris struck a deal with Ben Rictus whereby Ben would send a power surge into Kicker Charlie's at the height of the evening's regret, and in return Garris would pay Ben Rictus ten thousand smackers to blow on whatever.

Now that night was as busy as ever what with gambling being illegal in Beerlight and in the back room Kicker was rubbing his hands together at such a blur he nearly discovered fire. Everything was going fine until a maniacal burst of electricity seared through the paynose wheel and the players found themselves looking wild-haired into the turbo of a jet engine — chips scattered like leaves, alcohol hailed and all but Tudor Garris fervently believed that Judgment Day had visited Kicker Charlie's. The paynose ball had left the wheel at a speed immeasurable to the human eye. A beverage crashed through a one-way mirror and revealed operators frantically punching controls like Oz's curtain puppeteer. Everyone bolted, hiding under tables and repeating mantras normally reserved for moments of gunfire exchange. Kicker burst out of the back room and surged across the casino floor like a mime walking against the wind. Clambering onto the table, he filled out like a balloon, upward aircourses billowing his suit as he gestured with a cigar that was flaring like a firecracker.

'Unless I am sadly mistaken we are experiencing a minor technical difficulty,' he hollered above the roar. 'But if you denizens stay serene, I feel it in my black heart that we can re-balance the wheel and get back to our innocent recreational pursuits with a vengeance.'

But nobody could re-balance the wheel because it was moving too fast to get ahold of. Jammy Le Mot the head technician put a stick in the spokes and was showered in wood-shavings. Ever the opportunist, Jerry Earl pretended to help and all the while he was using the spin-handle to carve a delicate wooden swan from an old log. A rumour began to spread that the wind funnel created by the wheel would cause freak weather conditions in the Beerlight area. A five-year-old came to Kicker's and flew a kite. People who had just washed their hair came to the casino to dry it. Toward the end of the evening Brute Parker dropped in and used the edge of the wheel to sharpen his knife. Kicker Charlie's had lost all credibility as a gambling establishment. Early in the morning the decision was made to axe the machinery.

Kicker was later arrested for grasping the sleeve of a streetcop and sobbing openly. Ben Rictus left the power plant and went in search of a literary enigma — but that's a story. Garris never played paynose again. He'd made a bet with Lou Shallow that he could break the wheel at Kicker's, blow everyone else off the table and close the casino through loss of repute. Garris used the money to buy a luxury apartment and he only returned to the casino once, to stroll in rueful, Armani-clad reverie around the now-gutted premises. Nobody had ever found the paynose ball — that is until Garris's visit, when he slipped on it and broke his neck.

MOTORCRASH

Sally the Gat was called Sally till she bought an Armalite semiauto assault rifle at Brute Parker's all-night gun shop and started shooting at Billy Panacea, burglar extraordinaire. The first person to call her Sally the Gat was shot at such close range the cops drew a chalk body-outline on the ceiling. Everyone was surprised because Sally had always been such a sweet girl. Some thought Billy had led her astray.

In the old days Sally had been the simplest of car thieves. She'd go into a showroom and ask to take one of the items for a test spin, then drive it down the block to a second-hand place and sell or exchange at a pancake profit. People admired her easy style and she and Billy Panacea were separately regarded as kids of enterprise and initiative. They'd headline in the same issue of *Parole Violators Bugle*. Finally they met in the Delayed Reaction Bar on Valentine Street, where they had both ordered meals which were of frail health. Billy's burger was bleeding like a miracle. Sally's chicken sandwich had been inflated manually. Billy and Sally independently approached the owner Don Toto from opposite sides of the establishment and proceeded to throttle him. Their hands met around his neck — there was a spark of electricity. When Toto subsided to the floor the two saw eachother for the first time.

Sally's beauty existed on the edge of sanctioned reality. Her body was a three-dimensional relief map of the beaches of Southern California. Her legs were a grounding cord extending from her base chakra to the centre of the earth. Her wraparound shades seemed to be an organic part of her head. Billy was pinned to the wall.

Billy was wearing white dungarees and a bruise-blue jacket over a black T-shirt which said in bold white lettering THE CONNOISSEUR OF SLEEP. He looked like a million Mexican dollars. Sally was overcome with a protective desire to buy him a new wardrobe.

Over the next few months the two fit together like a brain in a kettle. Billy had never been so happy, and knifed anyone who said he had. Sally made him a jump-and-stick, velcro-covered outfit for scaling pebble-dashed walls. Billy bought Sally a double-capacity roll-on roll-off haul truck which allowed her to steal a dozen vehicles at a time. Sally would hold street-mimes while Billy punched them. They seemed the perfect underworld couple in all but their neglect to get shot repeatedly in slow motion.

Ofcourse Billy Panacea and Sally were openly ambitious in the bettering of themselves in all things non-legislative, and this created conflict in the relationship. There grew up a competitiveness as to who made the most money, who could run the fastest at night and which profession required the most skill. Pretty soon they were taking stupid risks, bringing home more items than they could ever sell and putting their asses in jeopardy.

Neither Sally nor Billy possessed morals which were nosebleed high. The Mayor had recently made a speech stating that all crime was equally repugnant, and this led Sally and Billy to consider that their professions should be interchangeable. They decided to swap jobs for a day, as a test to see who was more resourceful. Billy was a modern guy — he'd once shot a rat with a plasma rifle — so he was happy to get into this variety of deal. But despite herself Sally was full of trepidation. The great thing about car theft is that transport is provided. Burgling a house is like walking into the lion's den.

Billy intended to acquire a car by Sally's tried-and-tested showroom exchange method, so he suggested to Sally that she burgle the showroom salesman's home premises shortly after Billy made off with a vehicle. Billy promised to create so much havoc at the showroom that the cops would keep the staff busy for hours. Sally would have a clear run during the early evening — time for decaf and a donut. This seemed like a fierce idea.

Night fell like an unbreakable plate. Sally climbed

in the window of the relevant premises only to be confronted by the car salesman frying an omelette at the stove. Right away she knew Billy had set her up — he'd led her through the steps of the burglary so that the modus operandi would match that of his own illegal entries. When Sally was caught she'd get the rap for Billy's recent achievements as well as this one. As Sally beat the salesman into unconsciousness and tied him to the radiator she wondered how she could have fallen for it. Everything felt unreal, like a modern novel. Time flies when you're having trouble staying out of the penitentiary.

Sally's next stop was Brute Parker's all-night gun shop where she picked up a firearm powerful enough to send a man into space. There was a sneering new Ferrari 348 parked out front of Billy's place. Sally blew her gourd. Billy was watching the *Hairbears* when his apartment was shaken with gunfire — windows exploded and walls crumbled — the place was being reduced to a hotel. Billy was embarrassed to find himself calling the cops almost immediately — partly to confirm whether it was the cops who were shooting at him. He'd never given Sally a key because he himself never used one. Sally blew the lock with the semiauto as the cops pulled up — she entered the living room and fired at Billy, who dived like a pike — Sally filled the davenport with beans. Making her escape, Sally aired two cops and ran over a third in Billy's Ferrari leaving a mark in the drive like a fumbled pizza.

She was across the border before Chief of the Cops

Henry Blince could count to ten, and during this three-day interval Billy Panacea thought up a cover story, all the while shaking like a leaf in a shredder. He said he'd damn well asked to be shot at by Sally, as he'd tried to remove her shades against her will. Billy was put away for assault and Sally began a spree of armed robberies which stretched decorously from coast to coast. The thing is that Billy hadn't set her up at all and had in no way stolen the Ferrari — within seconds of Billy's arrival at the showroom the salesman had intimidated him into buying the vehicle for a hundred and fifty thousand smackers.

BLOCK WAR

It was a joke downtown that Eddie Slam's desire to kill everyone was buried so deep in his subconscious as to be hardly relevant. The apartment building where Eddie lived was like something out of *Metropolis* — the walls glistened and the tenants were pale. It had a communal rat and a clientele of crazed barbers who hadn't worked in years. Merit stars were awarded for the fastest and scariest whole-body convulsion. Eddie had to wade through uneaten seaweed to reach his door, behind which there was barely enough room to change his religion. He was going stir-crazy and he knew it. It was like being awake during an operation.

Eddie's only friend was the unrecognisable, Jurassic janitor Ivo Beak. When Eddie first met him Ivo was spending all his time carving miniature figurines out of frozen snot. His face could only be done justice by the glare of a hurricane lamp and his DNA probably resembled popcorn. He was so amorphous Eddie could never determine what he was wearing. When Eddie asked him to define a snail he described it as a 'small, hard, electric child'. Eddie had been strenuously teaching him to read and now Ivo had written a haiku of *Woyzeck* to save people sitting through the whole thing:

> Flying kitten — catch!
> Bugger goes mad —
> Stabs girl!

Ivo left this with Eddie and went to stoke the coal-gas furnace in the basement. As Eddie read and re-read the poem he felt a strange loss of gravity. The sky outside the window flickered like a dodgy computer screen. When god wants to reward a man, she first deprives him of all his reason. Eddie started lighting his cigarettes in the middle. He created a device which ate bagels, and trained his dog to shout accusations at passers-by. He wrote a letter to the *New York Times* about his eyelids, and claimed in addition that his earlobes belonged to some other guy. Eddie was barking mad as a hare and thus almost indistinguishable from those around him.

Eddie perceived the galloping drabness of his undead domicile with a new clarity. The furniture had obviously been grown in the darkness of a mushroom cellar. The black leather desk in the foyer had, it seemed, been surgically removed from a bison. And the guy down the hall once addressed him as 'Sunbeam'. Where was the life in this slobbery? The existence of a brain in the entire building was a matter for savage speculation. Eddie plotted action in his barnacle-encrusted room — something had to change.

But it wasn't so easy. Eddie tried to provoke mass arrests by anonymously calling Chief of the Cops Henry Blince about the dozens of insane barbers in the building but Blince came round to have a shave and left stroking his face. Eddie tried to evacuate the building by yelling fire but at this everyone burst into the corridors with cameras and peels of celebratory laughter. He bought a bomb from Brute Parker's all-night gun shop but the blast only succeeded in straightening out the north wall. He released a sackful of energetic adders but later discovered that they were being snared and roasted by the penniless residents. One guy gave Eddie the recipe for a sauce. Eddie saw another tenant stroll through the lobby gnawing at a toffee-covered snake-head on a stick.

For all the respect Eddie was given in this place, he may as well have been wearing antlers.

It was a habit among the inhabitants of Eddie's building to shoot at the communal rat for therapy and sport, but Eddie just pleaded with it to breed like a rabbit and drive the other tenants away — the rodent would stop and look at him with a mixture of profoundest pity and lofty disdain. One dismal night Eddie taped a pack of plastic explosive to the back of the glossy vermin and sent it out — he figured someone would strike the expanded target and blow themselves to hell. The rat shuffled off the plastic, swallowed it and skittered right back for more.

Eddie was frantically aware that he couldn't have an unstable rat in his pad and chased it all the way out to the Loop Expressway, shooting the bastard with a Norinco AK-47 submachine gun. The rodent crouched on the road and exploded like a gas truck. People ten miles away saw the flare.

After that, things got worse. Eddie was a gaunt, Perkinsesque obsessive. He swore he heard rats in the walls. Maybe the communal rat had taken his advice and bred — maybe the whole family was ballistic. And every week Ivo came snaffling up and waved a bit of phlegm-soaked paper at him, covered in scrawl. Didn't Ivo understand this was the tenement where god had died? That its destruction was a service to life-loving men and women everywhere? And if the occupants got a little cod-eyed in the crossfire, Eddie could take the heat.

Saturday night, Eddie told Ivo to piston over to the Muse Street movie house and pantomime someone with a life. Then he went down to Ivo's basement and chuckled as he stooped to adjust the coal-gas furnace. Like the rest of the building the furnace had been constructed when people were thirty percent smaller. Eddie easily bust the main feed and jammed it into a hole high up in the hollow wall. The rats would be the first to go. He'd sit tight an hour and a half for the gas to rise as far as the middle floor, then pick up Ivo's phone and call the rooms up there until somebody switched on a light, igniting the gas and blowing the roof off the building. But the sap had miscalculated — coal gas doesn't rise, it falls. Within an hour, Eddie

Slam was dead.

Several froth-lipped residents of the apartment building attended the funeral and Ivo Beak read *Woyzeck* over the grave, into which two of the frenetically convulsing mourners fell. Ivo's first novel was published a year later and he was hailed as a brave postmodernist voice. He dedicated the book to Eddie Slam, 'patron and benefactor'. Five years later he bought the apartment building, evicted everyone, and bombed it to a shadow. 'Ask not what your country can do to you,' he whispered, 'ask what you can do to your country.'

INTERLUDE

The Delayed Reaction Bar on Valentine Street was a popular den with the moody and furious. Don Toto the owner and barman specialised in inscrutable, undead snacks, and shakes which were so narcotically corrosive that spillage resulted in convictions for arson. This intense fare left its customers conversing in the crash position. Grandiose lethargy and insane belligerence were the order of the day, and woe betide the silver-haired gran who dared boast of her grief and frailty.

Yet Toto had not always been such a bacchanalian figure. He had been energetic and unsuccessful for years before coming to Beerlight, but after an arrest in Seattle for drive-by chuckling he had set upon a fresh life. The family fortune derived from his father's design patent on Mr Potato Head — this Toto used to acquire the Delayed Reaction on Valentine, though amid the froth-lipped delirium and blistering invective of the bar, he at first displayed a pious and subversive calm. Unlike the denizens of Beerlight, some of whom slashed car tyres with their teeth, Toto was a mild-mannered gentleman possessed of a belief in the common good and a normal hatred of the cops.

The change occurred when Toto read a newspaper article which estimated that crime was taking place at a rate of one crime every four seconds. Toto had always assumed that crime was constant — like ten or twenty per second — and the revelation of these four-second pauses fired his curiosity. Why four seconds? Why intervals of no crime? Like a scientist who agitates atomic particles to observe their behaviour, Toto decided to study crime on a quantum level by creating wild fluctuations in its frequency.

He was in the perfect position to do so. The Reaction was slambang on a line between Brute Parker's all-night gun shop and the Deal Street banks, which were regularly robbed at the point of guns acquired at Brute Parker's all-night gun shop. The line transected a mile known as the Beretta Triangle and Toto was up to his ears in thugs who exhibited a pop-eyed and bellowing menace. Without provocation the Reaction regulars would batter him with tales of bloody rage and stabbing daggers, and at the drop of a hat would yell in finely-crafted detail what they'd like to do next. A typical exchange would go something like this:

BILLY PANACEA, BURGLAR EXTRAORDINAIRE: I would like to steal everything, Toto. Leave every home on god's green earth as bare as the truth, for I'll have you know as well as I do, property is not theft — we are required to pay and pay, and that is sad in the short term and fruitless in the long. Why can we not exist like the startled rabbits of nature?

DON TOTO: Well now Billy, have a care. Go around with that finely-crafted attitude and before you know it you'll be button-eyed and deceased.

PANACEA: You do not understand, Toto. I would like to steal and steal. Until the world is purified and clean, Toto, picked clean and white like the glossy bones of a buffalo. And there will be no hiding-place for these ultra-monkeys who are not even worthy to clutch the hem of my garment.

TOTO: Simmer down Billy, I have a suggestion.

PANACEA: I tell you I will leap off a rumbling bridge if I do not steal something big within the hour.

TOTO: Well perhaps. And as for bigness my lightweight stick-on friend, I am not unaware of a two-fisted shitpile of a tank just waiting and oh-so-ready for acquisition.

PANACEA: What are the premises?

TOTO: The Magnuson-Kramer Military Laugh-In off the Loop Expressway, and in regard to firepower I believe we are discussing a 12.7mm turret gun for the purposes of anti-aircraft mania and two 7.72mm bolt-on items which will cause the ultra-monkeys you mentioned not a little distress.

PANACEA: I'll be there before you understand it. And as for the getaway it cuts out the middleman, like putting a cigarette directly into a brainfold.

Billy burst onto the street drooling like a hadrosaur, and so did every other crook who exchanged views with Toto. Anyone who entered the bar with even the dimmest notion to misbehave would re-emerge with an ear-shattering scheme to fire indiscriminately among praying nuns or set light to all that is good and free in America. There was a gridlock of hoods and bastards heading out for a kick at the legislation. The crimewave rushed up and down the northeast corridor, taking its boisterous toll on waiters and the innocent alike. Amid the uproar Billy Panacea was arrested for trundling a tank over a street mime.

Back at the Reaction, Toto consulted the *Parole Violators Bugle*, which listed recent crime and updated the figures. One crime per three-point-five. He had eliminated a half-second of peace — but he didn't lie back. Cloistered in the Reaction basement, he studied the evidence and planned his move. At first he had assumed the cop/underworld deal was one of mutual dependence but he soon came to feel that although cops needed criminals, all criminals needed was cash. Yet he realised that this too was wrong when he seeded a rumour that an amnesty was in the offing in return for a week of no crime. It took two days for the needy to realise they couldn't live off forgiveness and during those two quiet days the cops went from shock to grateful, easy laughter. They had no dependence on crime atall, so long as they were paid to go to the office.

Of course when no amnesty was declared the cops found themselves slaughtered at every turn. When they traced the crime fluctuations to Toto they squirted a squad of plaingarbs into the Reaction who stuck to him like a smacker to a rainpuddle. But by that time Toto was into another cycle of discouraging lawbreakers. A typical exchange would go something like this:

PLAINGARB COP: I don't mind telling you I could simply eat the concept of death and bloody murder. I won't be deeply happy until this town is a silhouette of smoke and embers. Can't you just see it my friend?
TOTO: No sirree. Order is important, or else we'll all be toasted in our own sin.
PLAINGARB: You don't believe that — just between you and me Toto, don't you wish something would break the monotony? Like a strangle-fight on a speeding toboggan for instance. Or a sudden lunging with an ornate oriental blade of some kind — I mean you must be interested in something.
TOTO: No sir. Bucking the rules like there was no tomorrow leads only to despair and the flimsy bridge to barking disaster. Grim caution, my friend.

After an hour of this the plaingarb would stick out his chin like the bony snout of a garfish and hide his face against the bartop, snivelling like a child. The cops never got anything solid enough for the perjury room.

The most surprising result was that Toto had become an A-class denizen. He found he could pounce on docile strangers and yell toxic sedition in the streets with the best of them. He awoke to the side-splitting hilarities of creeping suspicion and mob panic and branded the Reaction with his own signature of flamboyant collapse and carefree violence. Toto's antagonistic, harrowing meals gained notoriety in hospitals everywhere. He no longer messed with the crime figures as he had worked out the nature of the deal — to make a living by infringing on others. And he wouldn't have to seek the meaning of anything again, through the simple expedient of living in a miasma of gibbering, demented goons.

HARPOON SEASON

Harpoon Specter was a con-man so adept at manipulating reality he could fall out a window and land on the roof — if he could make a few smackers that way. His least successful shenanigan was to tell people unless they gave him what he wanted he'd sit down and break his own legs, then roll around shouting in accusational agony. Nobody obliged, partly because what he was threatening was an integral part of the average Beerlight cabaret act. But there was another reason. Because he wore stolen garments and went around demanding money, everyone assumed he was a lawyer. Always mindful of a scam, Specter began to play along. Pretty soon he got a call from Billy Panacea, burglar extraordinaire, who was in the overnight can for stealing almost everything from a house on Peejay Street. A week later Harpoon stood in the perjury room declaiming like an expert. 'Your honour, a burglar is the same as a door-to-door salesman, except that he wears a mask and arrives at night. My client went out of his way to remain silent during his activities on the night in question — he wore sneakers, avoided ringing the doorbell, even strangled the family dog to keep it from barking. He did everything so as not to arouse the occupants from their well-earned slumber.'

The judge was slow to concur. 'Mr Specter, are you trying despite all that's holy to tell me that Billy Panacea — who is widely known for having burgled the denizens of Beerlight beyond all recognition — is in fact a keeper of the peace and a protester against *noise* pollution?'

'You can quote me your honour.'

Billy was sentenced to twenty years and Specter's identity as a lawyer was sealed in reinforced stone.

But the next case was a fiery test of Specter's reserves — when he had the privilege of defending Brute Parker, who ran the all-night gun shop on the corner of Dive and Ride. Parker had had a score to settle with an arms dealer entitled Harry Puption. Harry had sold Parker alot of sub-standard fare so it seemed that Parker had set up a nocturnal meeting with Harry at the Puption warehouse and spilled the beans, blowing out lights, drilling Harry and generally making the kind of rumpus associated with blood-spattering ire. The cops, arriving late from another murder, found Parker on the scene with a smoking gun.

A key prosecution witness was the head of the cop unit who found Parker at the warehouse, and when the case came to law he described that event in finely-crafted detail. 'We were tidying up the mess at the Hurley murder across town when we got a call about the fashionable events occurring at the Puption warehouse. By the time we entered the premises Harry Puption was dead meat on a stick and on a search of the area we hit paydirt like a goddamn rocket — Brute Parker was standin' in a state of hyperactivity and foamin' all at the gob. I knew he was out of ammo as my torso remained in tip-top condition. I attempted to inform him of his farcical rights but at this he became exquisitely violent and stated his intention of breaking every bone in my body, including the dozens of tiny cartilaginous ones in my ears. I restrained him with the help of twelve other officers, all of whom are still miraculously alive and kicking, your honour.'

Unperturbed by the testimony, Harpoon stood and strode casually toward the witness box, almost subliminally fastening the centre button on his stolen suit. He paused and, gesturing mildly to the cop, announced: 'This man has rabies, your honour.'

'*Rabies*?' yelled the judge, and the perjury room was turbulently adjourned.

When the case was resumed, everybody was tense. The cop had been shot, and this had wasted valuable trial time. Specter brought on a witness to whom he had paid a thousand smackers in memory clearance. 'Sure, I was there that night,' said the memory man. 'I remember it as though it were only as bright as yesterday. Heard undeniable noises in the warehouse and went to investigate. It sure was creepy in there,

Mr Specter, and that quality became unsurpassed when I realised I was not alone. Someone was lurking to beat the band just outside my line of vision, and he made his presence not unknown to me by stating out of a clear, beautiful blue sky that he was at that moment wearing hydraulically inflated pants.'

'And is this monster,' said Harpoon dramatically, '*anywhere* in this room?'

'Yes he is,' said the witness assertively, pointing at the judge. 'That is the man.'

The judge called a recess.

'Now just what in the computer age are you trying to do?' said the judge to Harpoon in the back office. 'I'll have you know just as well as I do I've never even *seen* a pair of ... so-called inflatable pants.'

'Well that's correct, sir — but only a denizen of the inflatable pant community would know that you yourself were *not* a denizen.'

'What does it matter if I'm a *denizen* or not — get the hell out of my office!'

Back in the perj, the judge stated to the jury that the hydraulic-garment-wearing allegation was nothing but a red lie, and ordered that its mention be struck from the record. The incident had wasted three hours of perjury time — enough for Harpoon to brief Parker on his story. The judge gave a warning: 'Mr Specter, unless you stick to the shocking facts I'll need a haul truck to convey my disapproval.'

Brute Parker took the stand like an early Christian saint. The sneers of the prosecutor bounced off him like corn-nuts off a movie screen. 'Me and Harry go way back and I was due to meet him and talk in a gentlemanly fashion about a certain line in subguns he had acquired.'

'And is it not increasingly apparent that you took your own death-dealing submachine gun with you to this midnight assignation?'

'It is customary,' Brute conceded tearfully, 'in the home-defence business to compare steamers with one's all-too-mortal friends and acquaintances.'

The prosecution asserted that the rules laid down by the lawmakers were more important than Brute's gunpride, but Brute expressed the belief that lawmakers and guns were one-and-the-same in that both existed to be shot or hung from his belt. This did not go down well with the jury and the judge was surprised that Harpoon wanted to continue. 'You don't have a finely-crafted leg to stand on, Mr Specter.'

'On the contrary your honour,' said Specter, standing as Brute stood down, 'I can explain in just five of your Earth minutes what occurred that night. Let us examine the evidence. My godlike client is well-known to the denizens of Beerlight as a believer in gun karma — a belief which states that if you miss the first time, you pay for the bullets you waste by stealing your victim's ammunition. Now Mr Parker was found holding a Heckler and Koch MP-5 9mm submachine gun with a thirty-round clip. Only seven rounds were found in Harry's body. Parker was out of ammo when the cops arrived. Of the other twenty-three rounds only two were found on the premises. Where'd the other twenty-one go? And if Parker really missed Harry with two slugs, why didn't he take two of Harry's slugs in accordance with his personal philosophy? Harry's gun was as full as a Pez. There are more holes in the prosecution's case than in Harry Puption's riddled face your honour.'

Well the prosecution loudly objected, asking how anyone knew that Parker had started out with a full clip.

'Nobody goes to a hit with less than a full clip in a thirty-round sub, your honour.'

'Objection denied,' said the judge, bored.

'It is clear,' Specter continued, 'that my client arrived in all innocence at the gore-hung scene of the crime with only two rounds in his subgun, and on seeing Harry so drastically economised, was quite understandably distressed and let off a salute as is the custom in our fair city when mourning the sudden death of a loved one.'

The judge interrupted. 'You say Parker loved this guy?'

'Like a brudder,' sneered Brute, and within an hour was as free and happy as a lark. Harpoon was raised to the status of a legal demigod, and to his distress other people began stealing *his* garments.

Now the fact is that Brute had indeed set out with a full clip on the evening in question, intending to use all thirty rounds in the dealing of cod eyes, and the only reason he didn't take any karma slugs from Harry is he deplored his merchandise. Some reckoned Brute was lucky the cops' arrival had been delayed by having to clean up the mess at the Hurley murder across town, but Brute didn't think so. He'd also performed the Hurley murder.

BACK AND TO THE LEFT

In a town where bulletproof underwear is openly on sale, paranoia is regarded not as a mental aberration but as a way of staying ahead of the game. To the denizens of Beerlight the notion that 'you never know until you try' is laughable in its lack of foresight. Carl Overchoke was further ahead of this particular game than anybody — in fact he found himself alone. When asked why he was feeling so sorry for himself he answered without deceit that it was a result of looking objectively at his situation. So it was like putting fire to a rocket when Harpoon Specter the lawyer and con-man stopped Carl in the street and whispered to damn well look out — he had it on good authority that Carl was under surveillance. 'Take care you courageous son of a bitch they're onto you.' Specter walked quickly on and filled so full of hilarity he had to duck into an alley to laugh.

Back in the street, Carl hadn't moved. 'Holy

Christ,' he muttered to himself, 'the trash of my existence has finally hit the fan.'

Then he saw some guy down the block reading a newspaper in an obvious attempt to look geometrical. And there was a van, parked across the street — damn thing stood out a mile, plastered with legal licence plates. Carl felt suddenly disorientated, like Robert Southey trying on his first dress. The guys in the van mustn't know he'd been tipped off — he had to go about in seeming innocence. How do you do that?

For two days he holed up in his bug-encrusted apartment, where the facts of his predicament caused an obscure foreboding — it was like hearing gorillas in the next room.

After the initial shock he ventured out, settling down to the unfamiliar sense that his actions mattered to somebody. He began to see everything in a new context — he felt important. It was like a drug. Knowing that all he did was being recorded and filed, his every move was loaded with significance. He found he appreciated even the little things in life, like boiling an egg. It was like being in a movie. Just a walk down the street was a fiery jamboree of rich sensation.

As he went through his day he imagined the report: 'Subject bought two cartons milk at deli, bought head of lettuce, three tomatoes, crackers, pure orange — at 22.00 hours proceeded home via Chain Street.' This was great! He even started varying his routine, incorporating shadowy behaviour to give them something to think about. For the first time in his life, he felt that someone cared.

It wasn't long before people began to notice a change in Carl Overchoke. He had become a voluble, self-assured presence. He came into the Delayed Reaction Bar and ordered highgrade for a certain selection of people — different people each night — according to a covert pattern known only to himself. Everybody there began exercising strenuous efforts to understand this pattern. When asked, he would smile and tap the side of his nose. He acquired a huge, heavy coat and cut a much more significant and noticeable figure in the street nowadays. Nobody knew where he went home. And he made more mysterious phonecalls than the devil himself. People wanted to know what he was into, and pretty soon he began taking select personalities aside and telling them in confidence that if they weren't careful they'd die with a velocity that would surprise everyone. The shit was coming down, he said, for real. He'd stop strangers in the street and say 'It's on' out of the corner of his mouth. He'd rearrange merchandise in a particular manner and then wink significantly at the cashier. Even the lawyer and con-man Harpoon Specter began to regard him with a new and cautious respect. Carl knew something, and everyone but Carl was talking about it.

It was Carl's very lack of curiosity that made him the bullseye of cop attention. Even Chief of the Cops Henry Blince, who for years had been passing himself off as a biped, noticed that there was alot more going on in the way of conspiracy and funny hand-signals these days. And on investigating Carl he found him busier than a bastard in a rainforest. It was well known that the denizens of Beerlight passed the time of day in the pursuit of relentless deviance and paused only to gnaw at a snared dove or burn the mayor in effigy. Morals were flung like bails into the inferno of the city's cheerful and inexpensive pastimes. All this was harmless and traditional but Carl was clearly the calm centre of a more insidious storm. When Blince asked a regular of the Delayed Reaction to repeat what Carl had been saying, the guy spoke florid, whooping nonsense in a hoarse voice full of good humour and illegal sedation. When recorded and played in reverse, he seemed to be saying 'The best things in life are gratuitous, gentlemen.'

This was too big for Blince's men, who after years of undiluted mayhem had become almost undergraduate with misery. He called in the feds, who set up a sprawling and decorous surveillance network with the express aim of catching Carl with his mouth in the pie. Within a week they had gathered incriminating evidence the implications of which stretched beyond the human range. Contacts, names, beverages — everything was recorded as Carl wove a web of intrigue through the city, making signals and remarks which everyone professed to understand. From the first recorded day, he was stating right out that he was under surveillance — how he knew this the feds couldn't begin to guess. He spoke into phones without dialling, so that anyone in the nation with the right equipment could pick up the message and remain untraceable. State of the art. In a swoop on the Delayed Reaction the feds arrested Carl and dragged him out backwards so that if he tripped he would appear to be struggling and they could hit or shoot him with impunity. But Carl was in a state of bliss — the fiery release which accompanied the final reconciliation of thought and reality. This was all the evidence he needed. He lay back and let the public disorder wash over him.

People ran after the armoured van as it took Carl away — but they couldn't keep up. They'd never find out the secrets he had always been on the brink of whispering, or experience the festive revolt he had had up his sleeve. Were the case ever heard in the perjury room, Carl would have only said that the prosecution were out to get him.

I thought I saw him a year later in O'Hara Park — he told me he'd decided to shave his beard.

'But you haven't got a beard,' I said. 'You've *never* had one.'

He regarded me with a strange smile. 'Now you know why.'

NO MORE SORRY

Charlie Hiatus found himself on the corner of Ride and Crane at a loss as to who he was. He hadn't any memory of his life and affairs — all he knew was that he was a denizen of Beerlight. He looked up. The sky was as blank as his mind.

Charlie Hiatus sauntered up Ride Street, looking at the traffic. Someone unrolled a window especially to tell him he was an asshole who should die in flames if there were any justice. Charlie thanked him — already he was filling in the gaps in his knowledge. 'But there isn't any justice,' the driver added with a yell and accelerated away. Charlie thanked him again and made a note of it with cheery optimism. He strolled on, blessedly possessed of an innocence denied those with any memory of their behaviour.

On the corner of Ride and Dive he pushed into a store to ask the proprietor for any help he could spare. The store was jampacked with implements of destruction, and sat behind the counter was a big guy in aviator shades, barely containing his impulses as he read the latest issue of *Headshot*.

'I hope against hope that that isn't Charlie Hiatus who just walked into my boutique,' uttered the proprietor without looking up. Charlie noticed that the guy was flushed red, and shuddering like an LA apartment. 'Because if it is I'll take all my lucky chances in one strong hand and twist out his sputtering innards for their brightly-hued and decorative value.'

Without a word, Charlie backed slowly out again, letting the door swing shut. Bewildered and thoughtful, he looked at his reflection in the store window and was confronted with a head and neck like a stack of starch slices — he seemed almost to possess gills. This did not fill Charlie with confidence. And when the face of the murderous proprietor floated up behind his own, snarling like an alsatian, he hurried on with a growing sense of fear and unease.

Crossing the road and heading down Saints Street he was alarmed at a sudden explosion of gunfire and a guy running out of a bank with a Remington 870 pump. The guy turned to face the bank and, bellowing incoherently, fired ten chirping rounds into a guard who had come prancing after him. A car shrieked up at that moment, and Charlie leapt in, gasping gratefully as it screamed away with him. But no sooner had the bleak-featured driver glanced back than he slammed on the brakes, forcing Charlie out at gunpoint and calling him a 'mother'. The guy with the

Remington pounded down the street addressing him with a stream of blistering profanity and emphasising every syllable with a blast from the shotgun. Sensing danger, Charlie ran up Valentine as fast as his arms and legs could take him, dodging sideways into a bar.

Charlie was feeling as ragged as a seahorse. Only the bartop supported his tolling head. When he looked up he was confronted by a guy in a bruise-blue jacket and white pants who watched him with a ghoulish loathing. The guy told Charlie he would give him some 'cod-eyes', opened a flick-knife an inch from Charlie's nose, then strolled to the other end of the bar and regarded him with slow, glutinous laughter. Charlie turned to the barman. 'What's that thing when someone gets a knock on the head and suddenly can't remember anything about himself?'

'Death,' said the barman, his face a mask of disapproval.

Charlie ordered a drink, was signalled to wait and went to sit at a table. A guy wearing purple dungarees and a LEGALISE CHRISTIANITY pin stuck into his bare chest sat next to him and drank through a lead pipe from a steel tumbler — speeding like a fire truck, his cheeks began rippling from the G-force. Charlie noticed that across the table was sat a green-haired woman with a tattooed forehead, augmented pupils and what appeared to be a cylinder-grenade hanging from her ear. She leaned forward. 'Sitting here,' she growled, 'surpasses by twenty-seven square leagues all the various and graphic crimes you have ever committed.' The service here seemed to be glacier slow, and the patrons appeared to take pride in outshining eachother's lethargy. The barman slammed a non-stick tankard onto the table before him, and sneered like a skull. 'Stupid bastard,' he emphasised, and retreated into the gloom.

Drinking, Charlie was not encouraged. All the evidence thus far suggested he was an untrustworthy, depraved moron. He was adrift in a land of artform malice and frivolous assassination. Everyone regarded him with a profound, almost cellular derision. What had he done to provoke it? He sullenly expected his erstwhile life to end quite soon in a gush of puce brains.

The speeder put an arm about his shoulders and whispered in his ear, 'Strong rules don't bend but break.' Charlie was seeing things in the shadows. Was that guy over there examining a single raisin? Someone else seemed to be moving so fast he was taking out the garbage before it had been created. The floor was higher than it should have been. The tables were connected by barely visible strands of pizza. A little man cowered past a window, flinching under lightning. A guy at the bar was trying to remove his own face. Charlie could hear bugs creaking as they grew. The woman across the table slapped the drink out of Charlie's hand and said, 'Egomania is never having to say you're sorry.' The universe was filled with strange, garbled laughter.

'Wake me up!' Charlie shouted, standing quickly.

The woman overturned the table and approached him. The whole crew began bearing down on him like dinner guests. And it was as Charlie burst through the doors into blinding sunlight, the denizens of Beerlight baying after him like leather-winged demons from hell, that he remembered he was the Mayor.

DONUT THEORY

Henry Blince was the only guy I knew who grew himself as a hobby, and he was now so round he would have been perfect in a hologram. Presumably one of those chins belonged to his Inner Child. I know for a fact that as Blince outgrew his house he bought progressively smaller dogs to give the place some scale. And it was Blince's responsibility to simulate law enforcement for the Beerlight area.

Whenever a crime was accomplished Blince's men had to track him down at the Nimble Maniac, the Rainbow Takeaway or Eat the Menu over on Peejay and drag him like a reluctant cow to the scene of the inevitable. He would always be found frowning in the eatery, devoting his pre-Cambrian intellect to questions whose profundity were matched only by their acute irrelevance to the working man. If all roads lead to Rome, how can anyone who lives there ever leave? If music be the food of love, why haven't birds got ears? Why didn't dinosaurs put on any underwear? Were he and his dog co-dependent? This was the sort of thing that occupied Blince's mind. When he heard that Jackson Pollock had suffered a fatal car smash, all he could think was that nobody was better qualified.

When Blince was hauled off to Deal Street in the middle of a meal his amorphous frame was filled with anticipation. For this man every breach of statute was a foodstuff opportunity. He had eaten Exhibit A at the Mirsky murder, released a contagion of armed robbers when they offered him a taco and in a moment of desperation last year had swallowed a victim's wreath. The murder scene at Deal Street contained all the features we have come to expect in such circumstances, including a sobbing spouse and the much-debated stench of death — even the splash of blood on the wall was not absent. Blince slowly thrust his way into the kitchen and surveyed the body and surroundings. 'This the guy?' he growled, gesturing with a cigar at the corpse.

'You reckon it was murder, Chief?' beamed a fidgeting cop.

'I'd stake life and limb on it, Benny. Are we *all* made of meat, Benny — that's what I ask myself over and again in the dark hours. My god it's enough to dent your cerebellum.'

'You sure are one sick son of a bitch, boss,' Benny said cheerfully.

'You bet your goddamn life I'm sick — sick of you casting asparagus at my authority. Where's the goddamn wife?'

'She's here boss — she's pretty upset.'

'Your husband is dead, Mrs Devlin.'

Mrs Devlin blubbed like a seal. 'It's impossible, he can't be.'

'No? Well, then it's a miracle he is. Gedder outta here, Benny.'

'Right.'

'Wait a minute,' said Blince abruptly, stopping everything. 'Are those donuts on the counter, Mrs Devlin?'

'Wh ... why yes, those are donuts ... '

'I thought so. Husband had a habit eh?'

Mrs Devlin was bewildered. 'A ... a habit?'

'There are three donuts in evidence, Mrs Devlin — nobody leaves three donuts uneaten. Not unless they're cold-turkey. Or gorged.'

'My god, Mr Blince, my husband was shot. The *last* thing he'd be thinking about is *donuts*.'

'Exactly — donuts. Sidder down, Benny — we're gonna be here awhile.'

The scar tissue moon rose slowly over a city of echoing shots and bonfire cars. Throughout the night the two cops sat with seemingly infinite patience in the dead air which accompanies the stifling of fact — while Mrs Devlin was slowly crushed by its weight. 'Let's go over it again,' rumbled Blince. 'You created six donuts. Your doomed, misguided husband ate one of them while you stood and watched. You left, and when you came back no more than two minutes later the scene was exactly as it is now — that your story? My god, Mrs Devlin, you tell that in the perjury room you'll be dead quicker than an airplant.'

'But it's the truth you stupid man, the truth! How else can I say it?' And she broke down into sobs of quaking intensity.

'Let's attempt a benign reconstruction, Benny. As I see it Mrs Devlin there are three possible scenarios.' Blince got up and went over to the plate of donuts. He picked one up and took a bite, chewing. 'Your husband in all his fragile innocence, pausing only to offer up a prayer to our Lord, entered the blistering vortex of this immoral chamber in search of nourishment. You yourself, clutching at straws in a desperate attempt to salvage something — anything — from the twisted wreckage of your relationship, had deepfried him a doughy repast. Eating one, your husband stated his first-rate opinion that the donut he had sampled would never become what it ought to be, and cast shadowy doubts upon your skill as a cook, wife and lover.'

'I beg your pardon.'

'At this you became exquisitely violent, and gave your husband the cod-eye by means of a Walther 9mm automatic which you subsequently disposed of in whatever manner your damaged imagination could devise. Am I getting through to you Mrs Devlin?'

'You've run stark raving mad you disgusting tyrant.'

'Tyrant am I? Distorting the facts! Well, Miss Cherub in the Firmament, I'll have you know better than I do this round-eyed and refreshing simplicity isn't fooling anyone. Is this how you looked at your husband before he suffered the flash-flood of your arrogance and fury Mrs Devlin? My god he was dead before the donut reached his midsection.'

'But it doesn't make any *sense* you madman — '

'Madman am I? I'll fry you in sauce for that you crazy bitch.'

Benny whispered something in Blince's ear.

'What?' said Blince, frowning. 'Whaddya mean I can't fry her in sauce? Quit snaffling at my ear — I can do whatever I like in this kitchen. Didn't you drag me out of the Nimble Maniac before I was good and ready?'

'Please,' said Mrs Devlin. 'I *must* sleep.'

'Simmer down, lady,' said Benny. 'We're just tryin' to establish the facts.'

'You use saccharin or aspartame in these donuts Mrs Devlin?'

'Certainly not.'

'Sure, I bet.'

Mrs Devlin was lost for a reply. Blinded by hunger and lacking the intellectual fibre to misconstrue the facts with the care advised by the cop academy, Blince surged on like an enraged water bison. 'The second possible scenario,' he rumbled, taking up the second donut and stepping over the body, 'has you, Mrs Devlin, standing here with a formidable sawed-off Remington automatic shotgun, a bandolier of Hi-Power shells about your flabby waist. Your husband was standing — here.' Blince raised the donut above his head — it threw a huge and infernal shadow on the wall. 'Awash with alcohol and drugs, you and your oh-so-trusting spouse embarked upon a grim shooting match, using these donuts for target practice. Lacking the ballistic expertise required — or perhaps being all too expert — you blew every trace of life out of your husband's face and ears. Then perching on his chest like a harpy, you ate the donut yourself, snickering in the artificial light.' As Blince ate the donut, Mrs Devlin hid her face in her hands.

'God's shining earth'll go up in a ball of flame before you let fly with the truth won't it Mrs Devlin? I sense sickness and depravity beyond the human range, babyface — the random particles vibrate differently on *my* nostrils.'

'Better not use that on the judge, Chief,' muttered Benny.

'Whaddya mean? This whole room's made up of random particles, you bigot. So's every crime scene from here to San Diego.'

'But I'm innocent you nasty man,' shrieked Mrs Devlin suddenly.

'Where? On the candy planet?'

'Good one, Chief,' sniggered Benny, flushed with hilarity.

Smirking despite himself, Blince took up the last donut. 'The last possibility is the worst I've ever known.' He became deadly serious again, biting the donut and using the crescent remainder to point at the sink. 'Over there, Mrs Devlin, you and a passing vagrant were involved in a carnal assignation of the first order. Alerted by cries of animal lust, your sweet-tempered husband entered the room and interrupted your sin. Caught like a troglodyte in a spotlight, you pulled out an impressive Colt Python .357 Magnum with a four-inch barrel — your husband screamed at a pitch only dogs could hear and you let him have it six times in the head, bang bang bang.'

There was a moment's silence in the room, like the death of a mime but without the laughter. Benny coughed quietly. 'Er ... what about the donut, Chief?'

'Oh yeah, then I guess she sat and ate a donut. Anyway wadduz it matter — the bastard's dead. Tell the boys they can take her to the overnight can.'

'Right.'

'It's a bitter horsepill to swallow isn't it Mrs Devlin? Bye bye.' Mrs Devlin was cuffed and dragged weeping from the room. Blince leaned heavily against the counter and wiped the crumbs from his mouth with a gun rag. 'There's one thing that still bothers me, Benny — it's been nagging me throughout these grotesque proceedings.'

'What's that Chief?' smiled Benny in gleeful anticipation.

'Are certain species of fish neofascist? I mean some of 'em conform to all the criteria.'

'Oh, Chief, you're missing the point,' Benny laughed good-naturedly. 'Don't you understand that once again you have eaten the evidence? Because you are digesting the few remaining donuts here at the crime scene, you will not be able to prove even one of them finely-crafted tales in the perjury room.'

Blince frowned with this new knowledge, then began looking about him. He picked up the deep-pan and looked inside — six more donuts swam in the fat.

Benny snickered, gaped and started blinking too fast.

GEPPETTO

Leon Wardial was cheerfully ahead of his time — but it was a close call. As a student Leon had almost become English through bad illumination and lack of exercise. Noting that the precedent system in Western law bore an identical structure to that of mental neurosis, he had written a thesis on *Crime as a Creative Medium* and been kicked out bodily by a principal of such brittle health Leon himself had had to support him during the procedure. He entered the world with an almost senatorial lack of practical knowledge, naively invigorated by the dismissive rage with which he was greeted at every turn. Like everyone in America he wanted to make a living by writing trash. Academe had taught him that if you leave the dishes for long enough they'll get done by evolution. But Leon soon found that money had to be earned or stolen. Nobody wanted his thesis, which he had retitled *Damn the Police*. People told him the army built character, but fortunately he already had one. So he sought the traditional wisdom of Uncle Savage, respected thief and dagger artist.

Savage was stripping a chainsaw when Leon entered the basement seeking what he termed a 'burglar's wage'.

'A burglar's wage he says,' muttered Savage, a vein in his temple throbbing audibly in the small room.

'If you'll teach me sir,' said Leon brightly, tripping over coils of rope.

Savage looked as though he'd as soon shatter Leon's ribs as grace his ear with a verb.

'Can you handle a grapple, boy?'

'If you mean a grappling hook Uncle, no. Though I did on one occasion throw a net over a prairie dog. In New Brunswick.'

'A net over a prairie dog he says — god almighty. On one occasion he says. I bet it's an occasion you remember well eh boy? While I can barely sleep nights for all the wildlife I've wrestled into submission with these two hands.'

'Pardon me Uncle but your bestial peccadilloes are hardly the issue here.'

'What, you bastard? I'll slash your throat from sternum to navel.'

Bounding over moonlit rooftops, arguing red-faced over the plunder and bickering at the foot of their victims' beds, Leon and his uncle formed an uneasy alliance. Whistling loudly as he dropped silverware into the sack which Savage, glaring furiously, held open, Leon would reel off quotations from Voltaire in a Scottish accent and pause only to have a good laugh. He repeatedly alarmed his uncle by pretending to pass out on the premises and would wait until Savage, flushed and gasping from the exertion, had dragged him through the window to safety before sitting up and asking why Savage's belly was heaving. He became adept at snagging his uncle's pants with a grappling hook and hurling them at the eaves in a flap of rags. Pointing with a guffaw whenever Savage tripped on a slate, Leon was a constant source of umbrage and the two would inevitably scuffle and shove on the starlit ledges, hurling diamonds and slugging eachother with nuggets of masonry.

Leon had quickly discovered that the best way of getting into something is to think of it as mischief. This adroit principle entered him like a sickness. It suggested that the tedium of the getaway could be relieved by pretending that Kermit was trying to get out of the sack. It caused him to sit at gang meetings mimicking a cop siren without moving his lips. He made unneeded extra cash at K-Mart demonstrating flame-retardant dungarees. He frightened little kids by murmuring poetry. The cops hated him — he was forever telling the truth and throwing a spanner into their inquiries. Savage felt as though he'd knitted a monster.

But he had to concede that Leon had contracted a personality since the days when he had had to stamp on snails in an attempt to entertain the gloomy child. Most youngsters these days could not entirely believe in a thing unless it was printed on a T-shirt, but Leon seemed to have a genuine interest. Savage talked about his life as a re-offender. How could someone be offended by the same thing twice? Was nothing learnt?

Leon theorised that a thief creates something out of nothing, like an artist or god. These lisped absurdities made Leon unpopular with other criminals, and Savage suffered a loss of esteem by association. They wanted to know why Savage stood for it, and he felt the pressure. He began to think Leon was being resentful for the time Savage had tried to teach him about real life by dragging him behind a Chevy. Leon had been eight years old at the time and had made no comment except to thank his uncle for demonstrating the behaviour of a typical bastard. In truth the incident was one of Leon's fondest memories and in the autobiographical novel *Burgling In Beerlight With Uncle Savage* he attributed the whole thing to Savage having taken buoyant leave of his senses. Savage was a laughing stock before the book's publication but on hearing of its existence he lunged across the table at Leon's throat. Pulling away with his uncle's hands about his neck Leon dragged him through shattering breakfast plates and into a struggling, screaming heap, kicking over chairs and straining for weapons just out of reach. This scuffle formed the opening scene in the stage adaptation, which was notorious for the ending in which a cop appeared on stage and arrested the audience. The acclaim which greeted *Uncle Savage* came as a total surprise to Leon and a shock to his uncle, whose hair went black overnight. Disguised as an Arab and approaching Leon at a dinner party, he had barely begun to express his feelings when Leon tugged down his false beard, at which Savage retreated in alarm. They say a little embarrassment's good for you — I wonder what they say about this much?

Leon wallowed in the newfound popularity which was aided by his readers' fascination with the perils of his work. The lady host of a literary soirée once found her absent guest speaker burgling her bedroom and brought him downstairs in a din of delighted applause. Leon, flattered and bashful, removed his mask and accepted their toast, presenting the host with a crowbar and searing his admirers with a volcano of modesty.

Leon's idea of a perfect crime was one during which he enjoyed himself. How could he be so selfish? Crime was supposed to be a necessity — the cops didn't want people to think crooks were enjoying it, and crooks didn't want the cops to think so either. Leon was blowing the gaff like there was no tomorrow. He'd never been popular on the west coast, where bigtime hoods have the souls of accountants. But now even the Beerlight mob was brooding and Dino Korova the hoodboss hauled Savage in by the legs. Savage was not unconnected with the mob and so by association Leon was not unconnected any the more. Dino Korova did not like to hear Leon saying he was having the time of his life as a burglar in Beerlight. Night and day Leon was on chat shows stating the benefits of not having to pay, and it was placing mob rule in a bad glare. As the keeper of the Beerlight mob it pleased Dino to pretend it was fragile, and alluding to Leon's cool calculated cheek he stated with a yell that he'd oblong the bastard with an ammo-guzzler.

Savage found himself arguing on Leon's behalf with an almost forensic intensity. What with the hazards of drugs, sex and spiritual quest, crime was one of the few activities a young man could undertake without fear of the consequences. Leon's lack of unconnectedness with the mob was as slender as a bug's fetlock. The boy could walk down Chain Street picking both nostrils simultaneously with a tuning fork and no one would give a thought to the mob or anything else. And as a burglar, nobody was more punctual.

'Never was a truer word spoken,' said Dino Korova. 'At least not around here. I'll have you know what I intend to do with this skulking paragon, Savage — you two will enter a premises on my behalf, and if Leon begins chanting, impersonating a crash dummy in slow motion or braying with laughter during the job, I assure you he'll depart the world like a greyhound out of a trap. This joker of a nephew of yours grows more floridly conspicuous every time I look away. I cannot allow the national media to perceive the moral angularities of my enterprise.'

Savage tracked Leon down at a squash club and tried to impress upon him this opportunity to redeem himself or face the boneshattering music. Leon distractedly agreed during a slamserve and turned up cheerily on the night with only the dimmest notion of what was riding on it. Gasping with hilarity, he shuffled into the dark alley and began to mime an encounter with an invisible wall. Bristling with common sense, Savage watched as the evening developed into a fiesta of song and balloon animal mayhem. Leon proceeded as though there were no such thing as a burglary. The premises was quickly filled with semi-inflated dogs and volleys of abuse. Savage stood slack-featured and regarded the fading afterimage of his integrity. And then, as Leon began playing a trumpet, years of sedentary, strolled burglaries exploded like a fumbled egg. Savage saw with a pellucid clarity the notion which would transform his previously dreary career. Leon was bringing him on. Leon wasn't into misery because it lacked the element of surprise.

Neighbours were banging on the walls and cop sirens began to wail. Leon and Savage were on the roof, releasing balloon creatures and bellowing quotations from Poe at operatic volume. The cops arrived gung-ho for justice and hauled them yanking and flapping to the state pen at such speed their yells underwent a Doppler shift. The arrest produced baffling headlines which had to be qualified and explained at length, and then the issue sank like a U-boat. Savage was so happy his teeth hurt. His smug mediocrity lay cooling on a slab. Leon was out of the public eye and wouldn't have to be abstracted by Dino. The book continued to circulate, and would later enthral Billy Panacea, burglar extraordinaire. Leon and Savage were celebrities inside. And when the pen priest told them the walls of hell were four thousand miles thick, they began at once to formulate a plan for breaking in.

AUTO EROTICA

More murders are committed at 92 degrees fahrenheit than at any other temperature. How crisply I recall the summer when the thermometers hit the 92 mark and the denizens of Beerlight burst hollering onto the streets and began arbitrarily shooting the life out of eachother. For the first time there was a real sense of community. Everyone woke up to the fact that they were living in a barnacle-encrusted city run by a donut-crazed cerebral-retentive and a strange, gill-bearing mayor. It was difficult to tell where one bastard ended and another began, and the town was immediately swept by lucrative rioting and lush panic. Shrapnel flew through the air as if by enchantment. All minorities were catered for by the hail of lead and aluminium. Freddy Bitmap was assaulted with a rivet gun. Lester Mirsky was smacked by a truck on Crane Street. Dino Korova the hoodboss shot three of his best men with a Colt Python then turned it around and blew off his own unredeeming features. Brute Parker entered the Delayed Reaction with a street-sweeper and knocked ten people onto the back wall — it was like an explosion in a melon shed. My good friend Billy Panacea dropped by for a visit and stabbed me six times in the chest with a bowie knife — I'd never seen him so happy. He leapt screaming onto the bandwagon and in the following days took every risk available to him, burgling premises for all he was worth. Those cops not instantly dead and buried were stringently demoralised, and one escaped through the skylight of the beleaguered cop den wearing a vertical take-off jet. The mayhem had all the diversified and collaborative qualities of good improvised theatre and it wasn't surprising that the papers claimed not to understand it.

All that summer everyone had been critical of my death-defying attachment to Bleach Pastiche and the supposed idea that it ripped the balls off polite society — I couldn't even visit the Delayed Reaction Bar without Don Toto the owner yelling his view that she was poison. 'It'd be cruel to test her on animals, you clown. She walks around with a Parabellum automatic in her jacket — she's more scary than a cretin with a vote.'

But these observations ricocheted off me so fast Toto caught the fragments in his leg. Me and Bleach were burning like Shelley's cadaver and any ill-feeling I had ever harboured languished like a drying starfish. It takes alot to change what people laughingly refer to as my mind, though in the first weeks even I was baffled by the draw — she wasn't a beautiful mess, she was just beautiful. Her mouth was so red I had to regard it through a welding mask. She had a registered trademark symbol tattooed on her forehead and every accessory she wore was capable of exploding harmfully. She had dyed her hair luminous in honour of her twin sister who, starved of colour in the eighties, had finally blown her head off with a flare gun. Bleach taught me so much about the world — like how the atom bomb was the result of Einstein mistaking a roving flea for a decimal point in his calculus, that America produces better physical comedy because there's more room and that for a two-dimensional being 10 and 90 miles per hour are the same on a 100 mph speedometer. She once rubbed a sleep crumb out of her eye and when I studied it under a microscope I found it was a perfect miniature replica of an Alpine village.

Bleach existed in a colourful corner — her TV didn't get snow, it got sunburn. She moved through the Beerlight streets in a cloud of army surplus and drove a surgical-pink convertible. The back of the car had caught light in a bomb accident and everyone had joined in with wrenches and hammers to make shapes before the metal cooled — the rear wings were now rippled and stretched like a discarded rubber.

The cops wanted an audience with Bleach because she was responsible for seven important murders but in the four days that the atmosphere remained at 92 they were fully occupied supervising the violence. So what with Bleach's munitions knowledge and the feeling of invulnerability common to kids newly on the shaft we felt safe and inclined to go for a leisurely cruise in the exaggerated sun. My borrowed AK-47 sub lay in the back and I drove with one arm about Bleach and her S&W 9mm ACP, her Armalite AR-180 semiauto, her SPAS-12 autofeed, her M-79 grenade launcher and her cut-down Remington skeet. She kissed me like a frog and passed a pill that numbed my body and stopped the pain in my chest. We laughed in the knowledge that in the trunk were stowed a Panzerfaust-3, an adjustable dagger set, a Japanese bolus and a three-sectioned staff. Life was strong and durable as the wind whistled through the pin of Bleach's body-grenade. Parking turbulently on the waterfront, we felt like the perfect antidude couple as we strolled down the boardwalk with a golfbag containing the best of our home-defence artillery. We thought our passion would last forever, like styrofoam. Bleach elaborated on her theory about how Lee Harvey Oswald survived and changed his name to Bob Newhart, and we idled at a fish stall for a snack — but we had reckoned without the pathological climate. Instantly belligerent, the fish-seller formed his hand into a claw and expressed indignation at our breathtaking arrogance in requesting food from a guy like him. Rolling up his sleeves, he shrieked about how things were done when he was a boy.

A disturbance developed during which everyone on the pier pulled out an automatic weapon. Even picturesque passers-by walking small chirpy dogs became gun-toting, bellowing maniacs. A silver-haired gran rolled down the hood of a baby carriage revealing a SMAW launcher with a dual-function HEDP projectile and nightsighter. Taffy Moodswing, who ran the boat-hire service, ran screaming up the steps with an H&K, rapid-firing before a target had so much as graced his eye. Any sign of mannered deportment went out the window. Even as he was firing a Winchester the fishman yelled that he couldn't hear himself think. Taffy was slobbering like a primitive, strafing the pier buildings with a fierce and Freudian inaccuracy. Granny launched the SMAW and blew the north end of the boardwalk to matchwood — Bleach and I were behind a lifeboat and dwarfed by the wall of splintering debris.

The shooting resumed before the smoke had cleared. And when I looked around Bleach had selected the Norinco. She took aim with soulful eyes and wasn't atall cruel. She'd been shot in the arm once and said it was like having her picture taken by god. Tightening on the squeeze like a Grafenberg manoeuvre — the cords in her arm and shoulder moved like a river and the recoil erased any question from her mind. Linda Hamilton with a touch of Spinoza, a ballistic angel, her beauty at that instant was intravenous.

Bleach swapped the AK for the Armalite and, aiming, narrowed her eyes. Her nipples were hardened like acorns.

'This'll hurt.'

Taffy prancing across the fireline — Bleach let it go. The scene was like a Scorsese movie but without the pretence at moral justification — and the gore looked fake. 'You and the clown better throw down your weapons or any moment now you'll be zinc-eyed and deceased,' the fishman yelled from behind rubble. I couldn't believe he was acting so superior when all he ever sold were manually-strangled lobsters whose bleak features told a tale of unrelieved despair. I began shooting at him tentatively.

But I was no good and kept hitting gulls and surfacing anchovies. Bleach was appalled and we began arguing without restraint. We got onto communism as usual, and Bleach repeated her view that Russia was never a communist country seeing as communism is the abolition of class, and all they ever did in Russia was abolish the middle one. Finally she said she was ashamed to be seen with me and stormed off down the boardwalk, her white tanktop an easy sight-target as she took casual pot-shots left and right with the 9mm. She scudded away in the car so I had to walk back.

In town the firing had become more sparse and emphatic. Chief of the Cops Henry Blince declaimed from a balcony but the combined effort of his mouth, nose, arms and legs could not produce the level of authority required to quell the masses. Brute Parker fired at him boisterously with the same Corbray he'd used in the Delayed Reaction.

But within twenty-four hours the only work for the cops was in cutting down the hanged and wading through blood so thick it pulled their boots off. The temperature dropped dramatically — at 92 degrees there are murders galore but at minus 92 they're unnecessary. Even the mosquitoes were frozen. Parker tried to make soup in a cauldron of water, boiling his Corbray and spent shells. Everyone was ashamed at having shot people without arranging an alibi. As Bleach and I argued in the Reaction we were shivering so much our features were a blur. I compromised by agreeing to use BBs, which take people's eyes out no matter where you point them. But the whole mess had lowered my bridge in regard to Beerlight, its alleys and apartments full of brooding garbage, stoved-in TVs and shipwrecked cars, the air polluted by flying ammunition. Even the squalor was nuclear-powered. What was it doing to me? Pretty soon I'd be regarding the world through an infra-red grid.

And for the first time I found myself dreaming of a land far away, where I would be awoken by the clang of opening flowers and walk through apple-green fields full of small, inexpensive cows.

FAIT ACCOMPLI

Ben Stalkeye had a fierce effect upon chance — he had only to walk into a room and the probability figures would go haywire. The unlikeliest things would happen, but on the sole condition that he didn't want them to. This was detrimental to his work — every heist he performed failed through the most bizarre chance events. He could never make anyone understand or believe how there'd be another robbery in progress when he arrived, or the teller would be struck acutely blind at the moment he passed over the note, or the gun he held would simply and impossibly turn into a sweetcorn. It happened. By tradition those who make pacts with the devil have some success in life, so Stalkeye assumed he'd made a pact with god.

A benign illustration of his effect on chance was his ability to throw a dice a couple of hundred times and always have it come up the same number, so long as he didn't want it to. If he tried to demonstrate this to someone it wouldn't happen, because he wanted it to. Stalkeye was fascinated and appalled by the immaculate simplicity of his private hell.

But despite absolutely everything Stalkeye was not one to kick back and let the blistering inferno of circumstance reduce him to bleached bone. The logical thing was to find someone else who had the same problem, but who didn't want to accomplish any form of crime. If brought along on the robbery this party would influence the probability ratings in favour of a successful heist and thus neutralise the effects of Stalkeye's bad luck. Stalkeye would have at least a fighting chance of performing a hold-up with the standard odds.

After eight farcical years he ran slambang into a woman who was running away from Deal Street in a flurry of smackers and sobbing like a struck deacon. Stalkeye took her aside and she explained her plight in finely-crafted detail. She had been all fired up to make a small deposit at a Deal Street bank when she saw a gun sat in one of the bank's litterbaskets. She took this to a teller and was instantly given vast quantities of cash. Then the teller began screaming and the woman bolted as though checking out of a hotel. She had inadvertently robbed two hundred and fifty thousand smackers from the stockpile. 'This town is full of recidivists,' she sobbed. 'Recidivists and people of imagination. I just want to be good like a lamb or perhaps a turtle.' Her name was Gerty Hundred Ram, regrettably. But Stalkeye perceived in her an innocence which, if channelled correctly, would make more money than war.

He told her he'd by all means help her to make her deposit — what could be more simple? At the strategic hour he'd just pull the Ingram M11 out of his coat and rob the life out of the establishment. They went straight across town to a bank on Cardiac Avenue and stood in line. When they reached the front and it was time to start the robbery, Stalkeye found that he simply couldn't be bothered. He was mildly startled by this new complacency. Gerty, in her turn, was no longer concerned about making a deposit, but couldn't understand why. The two were crippled by a rictus of lethargy and finally had to excuse themselves and leave the bank, mystified.

Back at Stalkeye's apartment he calculated the distortions of the day on a blackboard as Gerty sifted desultorily through her two hundred and fifty thousand smackers. It was crystal clear that in neutralising eachother's bad luck at the bank, they had temporarily neutralised eachother's desire to do anything there. Stalkeye recalled how he had been idly fascinated by the patterns on the floor. The sudden absence of annihilating fortune had left him and Gerty in a shock which resembled heaven. They lined up eachother's chakras like a snake swallowing a pole. And when they got used to eachother, Stalkeye reasoned, they'd be able to rob a bank like any other couple.

Meanwhile they were growing accustomed to doing what they wanted without all the forces of nature strategically mustering against them. They could move about the apartment without harmful incident. They could go see a movie together without getting mugged any more often than the national statistics suggested. They watched street-mimes without laughing. Everything was as it should be.

When acting independently, however, it was back to the old days. Whenever Gerty went alone to make a deposit at the bank she'd return with at least a hundred smackers. And if Stalkeye tried to rob a bank, as he felt he should as the man of the house, he'd end up buying shares. Once he opened a gilt-edged account which would yield impressive dividends, and left the bank boiling with frustration. Gerty once laughed hysterically at the antics of a street performer and was too ashamed to tell Stalkeye about it when she went home.

Only together did they add up to two normal people. And it was with this certainty that Stalkeye proposed his gas-attack on the bank on Belly Street. Gerty protested that they had enough money from her visits to the bank and attempts to give to charity. Stalkeye let her disagree, all too aware that if they both wanted the robbery it wouldn't stand a chance. In most things they held opposing views, and their well-being depended on this balance.

But as the robbery approached, a new anti-crime campaign started up in Beerlight. Henry Blince pledged to halve crime in ignorance of the old Zeno principle that if you keep halving something indefinitely you'll never get rid of it. The alternative was to halve crime and allocate the more lucrative half to the government, but this had already been done with the result that public sector crime expanded to fill the gap. It was imperative to the average bank artist to steal as much money as possible to spend after s/he finished the prison term s/he'd be given for stealing it. The cod sentence held no fear for those providing for a family. So the new campaign consisted of relentless, guilt-spiked appeals to do something redemptive for someone other than oneself or one's family and loved ones. But disregard the crime families in Beerlight and all you're left with is the Beerlight cop department — the campaign was like Henry Blince throwing open a window and yelling, 'Lemme alone, bastards!'

Fazed by the lack of logic or conviction in the campaign, Gerty began to have a rip-roaring change of heart. She found she wanted the hold-up to be an exorbitant success. And it was as she and Stalkeye stood outside the Belly Street bank priming the M-79 gas-grenade launchers that Gerty realised this. She immediately tried to tell him but he waved her off. Stalkeye knew she viewed his heist dreams as an obsession, and thought this was a last-ditch attempt at discouragement. The plan was airtight and all that remained was to keep the odds at a standard level. Gerty yelled that the odds were screwed — they both wanted the heist to work, so it was dead in the water. But the hour was nigh — Stalkeye pulled on his gas mask and kicked into the bank. Gerty knew they were doomed — that the odds were piled so high against them it was a wonder they could open the bank door. She pulled on her mask and went in after him.

But the odds were standard — Stalkeye, too, had had a change of heart. He hadn't wanted to admit it to himself but the new campaign had driven a gas truck through the gibbon-house of his sensibilities and he felt as sorry as hell for the cops. The heist went like a dream. Stalkeye and Gerty were wading through smackers and lived together with a happiness which would have seared the skin off a less robust couple.

AWKWARD INSTANT

Louie the Garb was the most disconcerting man alive. He was like a grapefruit — you never knew what was going on inside. A couple of times he called me 'Sonny Jim'. Another time he slit his arm, pulled out a long and purple vein and said, 'What's this?'

Billy told me he'd seen Louie coming out of a manhole on Deal with a tub of ice cream. That's the kind of thing I'm talking about. Louie missed whole weeks by walking behind them like they were the facade of a movie set. He claimed he could detect tiny pastoral scenes in his saliva. He robbed a drugstore disguised as a giant wren. He walked down the street while manifestly asleep. He spent every evening projecting *The Magnificent Ambersons* onto his own face. Confronted with the most serious news or sternest caution, Louie would crease with a hilarity that knew no earthly bounds. Without provocation he'd admire you through tears of mirth, shake your hand, and slap your back while you were facing the other way. When people saw him approaching they were filled with a strange, unwarranted guilt and a dread of the unexpected. Everyone hated Louie the Garb and wished him dead. I myself once pushed him down the stairs to stop him laughing. One time he got Sammy Vale to deliver a violin case to Brute Parker at the all-night gun shop. When Brute opened the case a weird lizard skittered out, knocking ammo off the counter and scaring the customers. Parker punched Vale, strangled the lizard and called Louie on the phone, shouting at him to keep his monsters to himself. Louie stood on a soapbox on the corner of Chain and went into convulsions, juddering to beat the band until Brute remarked it was time he was discredited with an assassin's bullet.

Cool as a cucumber and half as intelligent, Parker called a meeting at the Delayed Reaction. 'I've had it up to — ' and he punched Billy Panacea in the throat, '— *here* with Louie.' Parker set up a committee to give Louie the cod-eye or injure him in a way that would make him know. I myself, being known to the denizens of Beerlight as a man of no fixed personality, was charged with the post of treasurer. Now since no money was ever invested in the assassination project I had nothing to do but sit back and admire the mayhem and that suited me fine.

'Murder in this town,' muttered Brute, jaded at the sheer bureaucracy involved in concealing a killing. 'You're damned if you do and you're damned if you don't.' The two factors involved were setting and transport. Because Brute wanted the whole thing to look like a random strafe he couldn't bean Louie during the nightly projection of *Ambersons*. And the only other thing that could be predicted about Louie was his attendance of the Muse Street movie house when they were showing an Overbite double feature — so Brute threatened the manager and gave him a few boisterous prods in the eye, telling him to show a season of Arquette movies. Then he acquired an old beat-up vehicle because he knew the best place to put a body is in overalls under a car with its legs sticking out. Nobody bothers it for days and when it is discovered the swiftness of the murder inquiry depends on the social standing of the murderee, this being indicated by the make and expense of the vehicle.

At the appointed hour Brute stood at the third-floor window of a tenement block across from the Muse Street movie house. He'd selected a GE Mini-gun with a fire-rate of 6000 rounds per minute, reasoning that if a thing's worth doing it's worth doing disproportionately. He had on a pair of mirror shades so big they afforded protection to his upper arms. He hadn't seen Louie enter the house but swore he was in there as he felt it in his bones — Parker always felt things in his bones because, he said, it saved space. Billy was going to keep the street clear by knifing anyone who came near it and Bleach Pastiche was going to feed the belt.

At four transfixing minutes past two Louie pranced out of the movies wearing herbal dungarees and a shirt that broke the sound barrier. Brute opened fire as though there were no tomorrow. The street exploded around Louie, who was pulling on an obviously rented balaclava. Shop windows erupted and waterfalls of glass splashed onto the sidewalk. Louie was walking expertly on his hands amid the destruction. 'Die, you Situationist bastard!' bellowed Brute. 'Die, die, die!' The antipersonnel gun thundered in his hands, spattering 7.62mm shells across Muse Street as he peered gleefully down the sight. Grey clouds billowed aside allowing us fleeting glimpses of Louie as he mimed walking against the wind. A water hydrant exploded and started to geyser. Bleach was laughing painfully, holding her side as she knelt feeding the ammo with the other hand — Brute was still firing amid a hail of scorching profanity and deafening invective.

When he finally stopped he lowered the gun and peered down, indignant — Louie was sat in the lotus position in the middle of the street, consulting an improving volume. Bleach and I were crying with laughter. 'He aint even sincere enough to get struck,' exclaimed Brute, gaping down. He opened up again, but Louie was nowhere in sight — Brute stopped briefly, then resumed fire when Louie drove past, from right to left, in the corpse car Brute had selected earlier. Again a pause, then Louie walked down the empty street, from left to right, convincingly disguised as Brute Parker. Throwing the GE impatiently aside, Brute drew a Dan Wesson and started taking pot-shots at the figure. Louie glided back and forth like a duck target at a fairground. Then he stopped, looked up at us with a childlike, preliminary face and inflated his cheeks like a rheumy-eyed blowfish. The whole affair was beyond explanation, like a beard made of concrete. Brute was foaming with fury, and lobbed a cylinder grenade with wild abandon — Louie was at his shoulder, urging him on.

Brute stood quickly, backing against the wall — Bleach and I were in a corner, incapacitated by mirth. 'Don't come any closer, you goddamn surrealist from hell, or I'll splatter your brains all over the wall!' There was an edge of desperation in Brute's voice which even Brute had never heard. Grandly stationary, Louie stood awaiting the shot. The air was so charged with static we had bits of paper stuck to our faces. Brute clicked on empty. He frowned, lowered the gun and tore off his shades. With every second that passed he was losing weeks of discipline forged while breaking bricks with his eyelashes in the Shaolin Temple. Finally he burst into sobs, and Louie looked upon him with the empathy of a saint. It was like a Jimmy Stewart movie, but without the vomiting. Two days later, Brute's mother sent a telegram to congratulate Brute on the mature reunion with his kid brother. 'To understand is to forgive.'

LIKE HELL YOU ARE

John Stoop amazed everyone by his lack of appearance. Without his voice this man could not be identified. He possessed the anonymity of those who are in such a state of health and standard opinion as to be almost undetectable to the human eye. At the start of any social encounter Stoop would have to state in no uncertain terms exactly who and what he was. His own mother didn't recognise him — one time he went to see her and she only let him in when he told her he was Robert de Niro. Finally he had to sing a nursery rhyme from his youth to prove he was John Stoop her beloved son.

Now after this incident an idea kissed Stoop's brain — perhaps the first and best he ever had — and he decided to experiment. He hovered through the fog and filthy air to the all-night gun shop on the corner of Dive and Ride and said hello to Brute Parker, who was gutting a rodent. Ofcourse Brute couldn't place him despite their twenty hazardous years of friendship, but instead of saying right off who he was, Stoop introduced a dud moniker. 'Damage is the name,' said John Stoop. 'Harry Damage. Five foot eight. Blue eyes, brown hair and a chin straight out of a graphic novel.'

'What can I do for you Mr Damage?' said Brute Parker without blinking. Stoop put a down-payment on a 40mm grenade-pistol, left a laughable address and breezed out, heart beating like a steamhammer. Suggestion and projection — John Stoop was a blank screen on which the denizens of Beerlight would be happy to shine whatever he demanded.

Stoop took the snail by the horns and stationed himself at the bar of the Delayed Reaction. 'Remember me?' he said to Don Toto, 'I am Tony Endless, who goes around stealing dogs for a living. Gimme a scotch with everything in it or I'll die right here.'

'Now now Tony, you stay calm and collected,' said Toto, 'while I build a drink which in no time atall will have us hooking you off the ceiling with a broom.'

'Put it on the tab or I won't be responsible for anything.'

'Right Tony.'

And now Stoop turned to his neighbour at the bar and executed a mighty plan which he would repeat on a dozen occasions over the ensuing weeks. Reminding them of who he was, he would give his victims an icy smile and state it all in a mild manner. Posing as Tony Endless, for instance, his remarks to Billy Panacea, burglar extraordinaire, went something like this:

STOOP: Your sanity's on the ropes, Billy. All I see you doing these days is punching dogs in the nose and re-breaking leg fractures in a drunken stupor. A bad telephone manner while speaking in person and a head unembellished by a brain. You must have a hole in your pocket — there's a rat on the floor. Ha, just joking you poor sick son of a bitch. Extraordinaire eh? Bloodless, baleful and tentacular more like. You're a seacow in its larval state. These poor infants might be mesmerised by your ragged credentials but not this joker. Going full-steam for the criminal nut-house, eh Billy? Who'd have thought it? It'll end in tears Billy. Tears and vomit in a rubber room. Pupils fixed and dilated, if you want the facts — and for what? For the purposes of pert insolence and carefree havoc — the most juvenile of hobbies. If I were in your state of mind I'd shoot myself to a standstill. Don't spare us — even now everyone here is making elaborate arrangements to deal with your death fumes. Billy's wan corpse on a blistering bonfire in McKenna Square. They'll be grateful at having been provided with a joy to feel. God knows they've moved heaven and earth to be rid of the unholy bedlam of your imagination. I wouldn't like to be a hen within lusting distance of your beady eye. My god the lard you must get through. Your father would turn in his grave and spike his own nose if he so much as guessed at your evil. And your hairstyle is clearly the result of a misunderstanding.

BILLY: I beg your pardon.

STOOP: Oh that's good. That's very, very good, I suppose you're just some harmless patron mewing and puking at the bar. Well you've never pulled the rug over my eyes Sonny Jim. It's time for you and me to kill kill kill at the appointed hour. Midnight at the Waits Warehouse.

Then he would storm out of the bar and leave his victim in a state of aggrieved bewilderment. Such an unprovoked litany of the obvious was known to the denizens of Beerlight as a 'Pinter'. It was such a common form of address that no one batted an eyelid but a mortal challenge out of the blue was a cause for concern and anticipation. Ofcourse neither Stoop nor the figure he had impersonated would ever show up at the appointed hour and victims such as Billy Panacea would grow angry and primal, calling upon the home of the erstwhile adversary and firing suavely through the open door. In fact Billy brought an antique Russian mace out of storage and accosted the innocent Tony Endless while at prayer, breaking his arm in seven important places. Sam Transam, whose business it was to sell insulation in the form of codeine, performed a sprightly shooting in Suede Street and ventilated El Henry after John Stoop posed as El Henry and called him an affront to bigots everywhere. Stoop posed as Billy Panacea and told John 'Kickstart' Kelly he knew damn well what he got up to, after which Billy Panacea found himself trying to outrun a Harley ridden by John 'Kickstart' Kelly. Babyface Terrier punched Chief of the Cops Henry Blince out of all recognition after Stoop posed as Blince and gave Terrier a stern warning. The Beretta Triangle was up to its face in a vortex of mistaken identity.

After a few weeks of this Stoop was sick and aching from constant abdominal laughter. It was such a change from the meek odyssey of his former life. With an ego small enough to pass easily through a monofilament gill net, he had relied so much on others' perception of him that his own life was semi-autobiographical. It was a blameless existence — yet now he was to blame for almost everything. He was overcome with a kind of mythical pride as it occurred to him that he had invented an entirely new crime. Supersaturated with the wired, life-affirming urge to rumble and cheat, he became bold.

The heistmaster Jerry Diesel was demonstrating to the riveted Delayed Reaction regulars his fluency in *Behlta*, a Beerlight dialect which consists entirely of the vocal imitation of automatic gunfire. In the middle of it Stoop burst in and said that he, Brute Parker, would have the whole bar know just as well as he did that Jerry Diesel was a deviant turbo-monkey who deserved to be sublimated with a knife. Then he clasped both hands about the throat of his mystified adversary. Diesel rolled his eyes like a deepfrozen sheep as John Stoop shook him, braying with laughter. When a few meek voices questioned these fashionable events, Stoop told them he could do anything he wanted, seeing as he was Brute Parker, fascist bastard to end them all.

'Like hell you are,' rumbled Brute Parker, and

Stoop halted as though preserved in a lava flow. Parker was standing at the door and exhibiting all the warmth of a burst blowfish. He'd dropped by to scope for the Damage guy who'd failed to hold up on the grenade-gun deal. Stoop let Jerry Diesel subside as the whole bar advanced toward him.

It was Anxiety Hall for John Stoop amid the whirling and expensive disturbance which followed. Bundling their nemesis into the basement and strapping him to a barrel, fifty denizens sat and waited for the scales to fall from their eyes. Nothing happened. Among the onlookers was Stoop, his silent sniggers making him tremble like a roosting bat. The man they had captured was Brute Parker, and he would never let them forget it.

DEBUT

Auto-Rhino was the living embodiment of Hitler's theories — he was never anything but amused by the guttural assaults he committed upon those more intelligent than himself. It seemed he had sneezed out an entire brainlobe in early adolescence, and what remained swam in his skull like a lone crouton. He counted as wasted every day in which he did not strangle a man.

Yet despite all these disabilities, there was a single smart idea waiting inside him like a statue inside an unhewn boulder. At the time of Auto's stay in the pen it was the fashion to punish crooks severely so as to encourage their assimilation back into the underworld — a process known as 'recrimination'. It was thought that prisoners should learn something before they escaped, and this often took the form of a popular correspondence course in locksmithing. The syllabus entailed one lock per month accompanied by make and twirl details. Every wing in the pen chirped cicada-like with the switching of pin tumblers.

Only Auto's cell reverberated with animal yells of impatience and fury. Auto was clumsy with delicate work as he was yet fully to master the opposable thumb — though everyone in the pen agreed that when he did, he'd do great things. In fact everyone in the pen agreed with anything Auto snorted, for fear of being the centrepiece of an impromptu garrotting.

Nobody realised how serious Auto was about changing his vocation. A cellmate briefly assigned with Auto had read him extracts from a Wardial novel in the course of sobbing for mercy, and Auto had believed himself touched by the truth. He'd reform — become a burglar like Wardial, Panacea, Savage and everyone else. But lacking the dexterity even to strike a match, he felt unjustly denied the secret of fire.

An instant after busting out with a group of other shitheads, Auto realised a way around it. As he shook the rubble from his ears and stumbled through smoke into the forest, he saw that with his size and strength, he didn't need to bother with locks and combinations. Even Auto understood that every crime is as unique as a snowflake, and that he couldn't help but set a personal stamp upon his burgling career.

An hour later, Viscount Strange and a brace of chinless wonders were dining in a room so full of filigree it appeared to be awash with earthworms. The guests took measured bites of amoeboid delicacies in an atmosphere laced with unintelligible, raging protocol. A butler stood by as though knocked upright and insensible by a semi truck.

The irony was lost upon no one as a semi truck exploded through the front wall and entered the dining room, flattening the butler before he could announce it. The driver was already yelling, but as the door fell open the unceasing bellow increased in volume and the source balked into view. It was some sort of primate in a state of primitive emotionalism. Ignoring everybody, foam hailing from its mouth, it charged hollering out of the room.

There was a momentary — and not unpleasant — silence.

'Benworth,' said the Viscount to a colleague. 'Be a lad and call the constabulary.'

Auto-Rhino bullroared up the hallway, crashing into a large glass swan and scattering dozens of crackers. What kind of a place *was* this? He thundered grunting up the stairs. Wardial said you could tell the value of a premises by dividing the diameter of the main stairwell with the number of circles described by the banisters, inclusive of the upper landing. Auto couldn't count and had not appreciated Wardial's theorem at the time, but now felt assured of a fortune and rammed the door of the master bedroom, struggling through the splinter-ragged hole and baying like a newborn hellhound. His cellmate had remarked with his dying croak that there was a floorsafe in this very room. Auto laid hold of the carpet and began to rip as though at a tenor's beard. Within moments the room was a scene of plaster-dusted devastation, cop sirens were growing audible and the safe lay bare.

After careful examination, Auto identified it as a modified extra-heavy treasury with ten-layer sandwiched five-ply drill-resistant steel, anti-blow, beryllium/copper alloy outer and relockers. He wrenched it out of the floor, staggered bellowing across the room and heaved it through an unopened window, its landing regrettably broken by the windshield and roofsparker of a squad car. Cops were streaming up the driveway as Auto watched pop-eyed and yelling from the smashed window. The safe was in pristine condition. Auto disappeared from the window with a snort.

The Viscount and his guests had reached the top of the stairs in hesitant silence when Auto roared onto the landing and sent them screaming down again. Auto glared back and forth, the veins in his forehead standing out like ill-advised volunteers. He slammed into the music room as a mazurka of lawmen pounded up the stairwell.

Auto was cornered and unarmed as he believed that anything which could not be said with his bare hands was not worth saying. His last attempt to kill with a rifle had shattered the observation window of a Seaworld exhibit aptly entitled 'Shark Encounter'. Auto began piling tubas and harps against the door, considering whether he was hungry enough to eat his pursuers. It'd sure beat the meals at the pen.

With the piano in place, he sat down on a stool. Gazing at the keyboard, he became gradually inspired, forming thoughts which the rest of us conclude in the crib. Potshots began to spatter the window behind him.

Beyond the barricade, Blince's men were weighed

down by defences and respect. The cop who took the Viscount's call had been paralysed with laughter and, after four gasping minutes, had finally recovered enough to mime Auto's harrowing visitation for the rest of the department, which exploded into hilarity. It was well known that Auto's subtlety was at a premium. But now, as the cops neared the music room, they heard an unlikely sound.

It was like musical scales. Piano exercises, repeating over and over.

In the perjury room, the judge was weary. 'As usual,' he said, 'this is the most appalling crime I have ever encountered. This guy didn't have the common courtesy to wait for night to fall or the occupants to go out to lunch. I say that grade of insolence calls for life and change.'

Auto stood in the dock, drumming his fingers on the sill.

Harpoon Specter argued for a sentence as light as a dandelion seed, pointing out that human body cells replace themselves every six months and that when such time had elapsed the authorities would be holding the wrong guy. To his surprise the court agreed and decided to gas Auto before such a transformation could occur.

Strapped and silent in the killing jar, Auto held his breath. Everyone watched as the gas filled the chamber and Auto tensed as though giving birth. He busted his restraints, remained calmly seated and, gazing at his accusers, struck a match.

REPRISE

In his tender years Henry Blince went to sea and was punished repeatedly for his slack appearance. All anyone remembered of him was a belly and a vest. They sat him in a corner with a pile of potatoes and an order to get peeling. When the skipper dropped by to check his progress, the potatoes were gone and Blince could only move his eyes.

'Jesus Christ you aint tellin' me you *ate* 'em all?'

'Indeed sir,' Blince remarked, with difficulty. 'I am proud to say that I have.'

'There aint nuthin' to be *proud* of, you bigot! God al*mighty*!'

Now he sat in the Nimble Maniac on Breed Street, the inside of his head roiling like a lava lamp. What about hippos — was it possible that their teeth were simply stubs of chalk? If tortoises lived so long, why didn't they learn to speak up? Do trout cry? Blince shook his head grimly. There was still so much he didn't know.

As he bit into the next sandwich, Benny the trooper entered the eatery. 'Been a prod in the right direction on Pill Street, Chief.'

'Stabbing? Get a man to the scene Benny — tell him to hover gaping like a paddlefish till we get there. This pastrami's dynamite.'

On arriving at the premises they detected a guy who was bristling with knives and strung by the legs from a ceiling pipe. The kitchen floor was an action painting of bodily fluids.

Blince gestured with a cigar. 'This is the most gruesome offence I've seen since we got out of the car, Benny,' he rumbled. 'When you see someone hanging by the leg with his eyes closed it's six two and even that he aint alive.'

'Or aint proud, Chief.'

'You bet your sweet life.' Blince shoved the stiff into a slow spin. The effect was impressive. 'Get a loada that.'

As the cop photographer finished up, Blince expressed his regret that he hadn't a sea rod to pose with. He was still laughing when a kid wandered in.

'Pizza boy.'

'Who let this kid in here?'

'It's a kid with a pizza, Chief,' said Benny with mirth and patience. 'A *pizza boy*.'

'I'll be the judge of that, Benny.' Blince swiped the pizza from the startled kid, ate a piece and spat. 'This pizza's been thinned with turpentine! That how *he* liked it?' Blince gestured sharply at the cadaver.

The kid gaped and swallowed, speechless. Blince drew himself to his full height, and pushed the door firmly closed. He approached the kid like a Goya giant, blocking out the light.

'What's in the sportsbag, kid — a Parabellum? Cover me, Benny ... Well, get this. Kid's walkin' round with a jar of maraschino cherries.'

'Tell me you're kidding.'

'Guess you got some explaining to do, *pizza boy*.'

'Sir?'

'Well aint that sweet. Kid returns to the scene of the crime with a cherry jar and an attitude of respect.' Blince let out a sigh which resembled the wheezing of stomach gas from the recently dead.

'Looky here Chief,' said Benny, at the stove. 'Fresh char over the burners. Oven's cool. Guess that rules out a pizza.'

'Hold your horses, Benny. This here pizza's as warm as a baby's backside — no reason to think the first was any cooler. The guy didn't reheat a thing. And those scorchmarks resemble blast-burns from a Mac-10.'

'Well now Chief, a Macky's pretty accurate.'

'Not with a kid at the helm, Benny — in a state of panic. You believe gun nuts braggin' they take the head off a termite at twenty yards?'

'Better not say that to the boys at ballistics, Chief.'

'The boys at ballistics can bite my ass. Don't I enter the lab to find I'm welcome as an adder on a narrow ledge? All cos I caught 'em namin' rats in the basement. Every one of 'em's a fairy in ballistics.'

'Coulda been suicide, Chief.'

'If he'd fixed the pizza himself I'd agree with you Benny, but as it is he hadn't a motive.' Blince reminded him of the Beerlight rules for Russian Roulette. A group of people sit around a table on which rests a fully loaded gun. The first one to pick it up and shoot himself is the Russian.

Benny sniggered silently, turning puce. 'You'll be the death of me, Chief,' he gasped.

'What's your name, pizza boy?'

'Timmy Bedlam, sir.'

'Timmy Bedlam he says. How old are you Timmy?'

'Twelve, sir.'

'Twelve, no less. How long you been in the pizza trade?'

'A week, sir.'

'And this is your second delivery to this address isn't it Timmy.'

'No sir.'

'How d'you figure that?'

Timmy stared up at him like a hooked bream.

'Lemme reconstruct the fashionable events which occurred here,' said Blince, re-lighting his cigar. 'It's the old, old story. The porcupine orders a pizza, which is brought to him by little Timmy, a child of evil masquerading as a pizza boy. Sampling the merchandise, our topsy-turvy friend finds it is fit only for the military and states his intention of expressing dismay to everyone this side of the international dateline. Timmy, I can only imagine the vortex of sick fear and insanity which thundered in your brain like bugs in a drum. Your boss was just about at the end of his tether with your persistent unexplained lateness, verbosity, downright rudeness and threatening aspect, and you could not afford this brand of attention. The victim must have wondered what the world was coming to as he was bound like a hog at the point of a Macky 10 and forced to eat the rest of his funeral dinner, after which he was sublimated by a medley of gunshots. Fearing you'd awake to strobe-lights and the word "surrounded", you stood on — this chair here — and began to feverishly pry out the ammo in an attempt to confuse the evidence. Guilty as hell, your sins stacked up like vertebrae, you mistook the skitter of a passing rodent for the approach of an innocent neighbour and fled the premises leaving the corpse in the condition we see this evening, jampacked with kitchenware.'

'So why'd he come back, Chief?' asked Benny, as Blince finished eating the pizza he had roundly condemned.

'Wanna tell him, kid?' asked Blince, wiping his hands on his shirt. Tears trembled on the brink of Timmy's eyes. Blince took it as a no. 'The fact is, Timmy's scheme was deeply flawed. Paperwork at the pizza house would note a delivery shortly before the time of death. Timmy realised he would have to leave an uneaten pizza on the premises to conceal the shocking facts of the homicide — it had to seem as though the victim had never touched the merchandise Timmy had delivered. But amid the onrushing nightmare he didn't suspect the cops'd already be on the scene. We've broken this case beyond repair.'

'But ... '

'Forget it kid, we thought of everything. Tell the boys in the hall, Benny.'

'Right.'

'This was an airbreathing mammal, kid — it didn't need a blowhole.' The kid was yanked thrashing and squealing from the room.

'Seems to me, Benny,' said Blince, sitting heavily on a chair and taking a new cigar from his shirtpocket, 'that if a guy didn't have an internal skeleton, then when he died he'd produce no fossil remains, and it'd be impossible to tell how long folk of that nature have been roaming this Earth.'

Benny did not reply.

'What, am I talkin' to myself here?'

'Oh, Chief, do I gotta spell it out? Don't you *know* what you've done?' Benny was amused and incredulous.

'Well for god's sake break it to me Benny before my ears explode.'

'It is the plain fact that unless we detect an uneaten pizza here on the premises we cannot support the kid's return to the crime scene, and subsequently he will never enter a correctional facility and undergo his induction into the underworld.'

'Did I eat the evidence again?'

'You know you ate it Chief. For god's sake, you even ate the box.'

'I guess I did, at that. Now just simmer down, Benny, simmer down.' Blince went and poked his head out the door. 'Hey — they booked the kid yet?'

The boys in the hall were barely visible through fingerprint dust. 'Yeah Chief. Van just left.'

Blince returned to his chair, looking thoughtful. There was a moment's silence.

'So whatta we do now, Chief?'

Blince lit his cigar. 'Send out for pizza, Benny.'

PERFORMANCE

Billy Panacea, burglar extraordinaire, broke out of the state pen disguised as his mother. The escape occurred during the metalshop open day — Billy unveiled a giant steel effigy of Lenin and in the ensuing uproar Billy and his Ma switched garb and Billy walked out as happy and free as a lark. The plan ended there and it was as he entered the Delayed Reaction that Billy remembered his Ma, who found herself locked in the state pen unable to convince anyone she wasn't Billy Panacea but Billy Panacea's mother.

'Ah, quit foolin' Billy,' shouted her cellmates. 'You wanted to sail that notion why didn't you swap clothes with your Ma durin' the Lenin riot?' And they began to laugh.

Meanwhile in the Delayed Reaction Bar, Don Toto the barman was squinting and hesitant. 'Is that you, Ma Panacea? Billy aint here, he's in the state pen, remember?'

'I *am* Billy,' whispered Billy Panacea. 'Gimme a scotch with everything in it.'

'Billy Panacea you sick dog, your sweet mother won't take kindly to you donning a dress and getting blurred in the afternoon.'

'Ma Panacea is in the state pen,' Billy explained, 'and I cannot afford to be seen drunk or sober in my own garb. I must pass myself off as Ma till I figure a plan to bust her out. What kind of tricks does Ma get up to these days?'

Toto told Billy that Ma Panacea was due to judge the bakery contest that very afternoon. Billy threw back his scotch and bolted out of the bar before anyone could knife him to a stop.

Billy selected a cake which had clearly collapsed in despair. 'This cake,' he announced to the assembled hags, gesturing at the blunder, 'is the most excellent item I have ever confronted. In fact I fully and clearly intend to take it home and swallow it, before it rises.'

In the visiting room the following day, Billy slipped the cake under the partition. 'Here, Ma — save it for later.'

'The hell I will.'

'There is a file in the pie, you sick old woman.'

'Trying to poison me, eh?' she nodded without surprise. 'With a lump of metal. You never were one for subtlety, William.'

'Don't call me William, Ma,' whispered Billy, 'or I'll bust you in the eye.'

'Killing your Ma while dressed in her summer clothes. You sure are the last word in perversity.'

'Shut your face a minute, Ma,' said Billy with a hushed urgency, glancing at a guard. 'I intend to blast you out of here with a quantity of dynamite which will surprise everyone. In three days you will receive delivery of a large, hardbound Updike novel. The guards will not examine this, knowing it cannot contain anything of interest. Between the boards you will find the quantity of sherbet to which I have just alluded, and with which you will minimalise the east wall.'

However, when the time came the guards were so uninterested they tossed the novel into the incinerator, causing a blast which gutted the postroom.

So Billy advised his Ma to construct a huge DNA helix during metalshop and utilise it as a ladder to an upper window. Due to the controversy over Billy's last exhibit, Ma Panacea was forced to undertake a patriotic subject as an act of atonement — so she made the DNA that of a hardline Republican senator, only to find that the genetic irregularities involved rendered the helix unusable as a climbing frame.

So Billy set up a Noah break. By releasing twenty berserking apes into a slammer it is simple enough for the escapee, disguised as a chimp, to be rounded up and shipped out with the general herd. But inevitably bad communication led Ma Panacea to create a walrus outfit instead of that of the appropriate animal, thus appearing limpidly conspicuous amid the shrieking primates.

Billy gave up and resolved to get himself caught. He carried out a jewel robbery which only he could have performed, involving infra-red scanning, knee-hanging acrobatics above a pressure-sensitive floor, computer hacking through a gauntlet of alarm systems and a take-off from a domed roof in a prefab autogiro. When he headed out to confess the next morning he found that Joe Solitary had already claimed applause for the job, his beaming visage splashed across the front pages. He had wasted a robbery and couldn't afford the rap for more.

Billy was tired and angry at having to conduct business dressed as his mother — he'd trip on the garb and drop his burglar tools, sliding down the roof and into a lawnpool or the porch of a doghouse. He decided to go about as a priest for a while — at least this way he could wear black and beg for mercy without arousing suspicion. It was lucky he used this disguise next time he visited his Ma, as it seemed someone had got his description as he fell from a roof one evening and Ma Panacea was now wanted for housebreaking.

'Thankyou William,' said his mother in the visiting room. 'Required dead or alive by the cops and here I am in the state pen.'

'Pretend you're confessing, Ma,' hissed Billy.

'I don't need to pretend, William. I confess I'd like to slaughter you at the nearest and dearest opportunity.'

'That's good, Ma — don't lose heart. I'll have you out of here before you can say knife.'

'Knife, William.'

'That's the spirit, Ma,' chuckled Billy, getting up to leave.

The plan was this. Billy would pose as the head of an

experimental theatre group and blast her out during an in-stir performance of a play entitled *Billy's Ma Busts Out of the Facility Just When They Least Expect It.* This scheme had been a last resort for escapees since Leon Wardial printed a blueprint text under the title *[state name] Busts Out of [state premises] [Without Warning/ Bang On Time/In a Hurry/Real Slow/Other].* Wardial had seen nothing irresponsible in the publication, knowing there is no such thing as a dangerous book. For the most part, the play is a stark conversation piece. The set consists of a kitchen, the backdrop of which covers a pen wall of no more than two feet thickness with blast-through access to the free world. There's a table, chairs and a stove at the rear. A handful of mild-mannered characters enter and begin to discuss the whole question of ethics in modern society. One amicably suggests that crime will cease when people no longer feel a need for it, and he is roundly condemned. The question boils down to a jokey experiment to determine how the day's environment effects the average Joe. A volunteer from the audience is asked to climb into the oven. As soon as the volunteer is out of sight, there is an explosion of activity on stage — brawls erupt, characters laugh and yell out of context, honking clowns appear in miniature cars, farts are ignited, strippers of every sex burst into view, Ambrose Bierce is exhumed from a soilbag, some kind of election takes place, guns are blasted over the heads of the audience — anything and everything to distract the onlookers from the sap in the oven. Behind the stove, explosive bolts have been fired, blowing a hole in the wall — by the time the warden recognises that the play is not legitimate even by east coast standards, the escapee is springing over the state line.

The work had been performed twice before, but by players so stricken with panic and stress that the text had been either forgotten or delivered in unearthly, warbling shrieks. Billy was sure that a controlled performance would not ring alarm bells.

Yet Billy's Ma had quickly become a popular figure in stir by teaching all and sundry a blackjack scam counting tens to plus and minus round a zero base. The whole point of the oven stunt was that only someone in the know would volunteer — but when the time came a couple of dozen convicts stepped up. Ma Panacea had told all her new pals about the break and she herself wasn't going till they were safely on the outside. Billy had to wing it, ushering a string of inmates through the confetti-blasted onstage bedlam. Clowns repeatedly hurled themselves at the stove in a sobbing attempt to conceal the flapping false door. By the time Ma Panacea had crawled to freedom, the audience had been treated to the most baffling spectacle since Chaplin attempted jest. Billy dropped a gas grenade, waved goodbye and climbed into the oven.

The symbolic implications of these events have been the subject of endless debate, not least because there was not a single legitimate convict among the escapees. All twenty-seven were convicts' mothers.

AMBIENT

Nature hates a vacuum and tends to fill it with the standing idle. In this regard, Jesse Downtime was amid the throng but not of the throng. Sure, he once fell asleep while he was surfing, he used his only nervous thought to shave the stubble from his chin and his conversation was time-lagged as though beamed via satellite. But that didn't mean he wasn't up to anything. Jesse was an ambient, a specialist among the goons and antidudes who used the city as a crime studio. In fact he had honed his villainy to such an art he was practically innocent.

The road to Jesse's vocation was thorny and progressively narrow. His regular thieving career had been as shortlived as an epileptic snake-handler. Jesse believed that indiscriminate theft was an expressive species of religious abandon. He knew material wealth couldn't be taken with you when you die, so he made sure he was never shot as he fled the crime scene. But he hadn't the first idea how to raid a store — he figured it was common practice to just swan in and then stagger out under the weight of the register, sustaining double hernias and vessel-busts at which doctors marvelled and repeated the word 'textbook' over and over. He never neglected to wear a mask, but always chose the same one — storekeepers would hit the alarm the instant Daffy pranced in. He thought of becoming a good old-fashioned pickpocket. Pickpockets generally avoid Beerlight for fear of laying hands on the sodden and boss-eyed lungfish which denizens carry as a deterrent, though minimal research revealed to Jesse that many such denizens had forgotten the motive for this practice. There was a gap in the market — but the first victim Jesse dipped was walking so fast Jesse tore off his pants. He returned to shoplifting and began to boost midsize hardware items such as sheet glass and cans of primary vinyl. He tried smashing the glass and walking out with the pieces clinking in his coatpockets. He tried drinking the paint and flattening the cans, but the security guy would become instantly apprised and unsympathetic as Jesse began to gag and point at the can-stacks. The old scams never worked for Jesse and so he set upon a methodical course of experimentation. Individual licks of paint would leave the hardware store, clinging to Jesse's shirt. Outside, he would explode with hilarity and mischief. He tore the stalk from an apple at the deli and bolted, turning a corner and adopting a casual gait as, sniggering, he passed a cop. The loot became smaller and smaller. He began swiping lint from affronted strangers. He hacked a single bladder-pimple from a seaweed drift and fled the bay in a Cherokee jeep. He nocturnally vaulted into the state zoo and kidnapped a young ant from some undergrowth near the chimps. Then he returned it uninjured to the baffled authorities with a note taped to the matchbox: 'NOTHING COULD BE EASIER, LOSERS'. No one could believe or detect his daring. He could steal the angels from the head of a pin. Even his aura was not his own. He'd stumble into people on the street, acquiring dozens of their atoms without suspicion. Crossing the Mexican border, nobody suspected he was smuggling salty tears within his concealing head. A pioneer of the small but perfectly-formed offence, he was abruptly arrested in a restaurant on Dive Street, his nose packed full of sub-atomic particles. By the time Jesse was released, he had refined his crimes to such a degree that they occurred only as electrical impulses at the synapses of his brain. Surely no one could tell him what to think?

But this was America.

AUNT MAGGOT'S LEGACY

Aunt Maggot died in violent and hilarious circumstances over which I will sling a veil — what is important is that she left behind a fortune to a tune which burst the eardrums of the Beerlight community. Maggot's riches surprised her associates for she was thought to be as honest as a high summer day. Billy Panacea, burglar extraordinaire, wept openly when he heard the news. But it seemed he and others were to have a shot at the cash anyway, as Maggot had written half a dozen bigots into her will. Billy was her nephew but the rest only knew her as Billy's aunt and had tried, in their way, to treat her with respect. The will was a creepy notion as Maggot was a believer in the afterlife and had once attempted to contact her late husband through a masseur. Billy, Parker, Toto, Harpoon, Bleach and Gilbert Wham assembled in the oak-panelled office of Maggot's attorney. Parker wore a suit. The group sat around the table feeling as comfortable as a giraffe in a trashcan.

The attorney, Mr Pert, was an expensive relic of his former self. He was the type who would act all high and mighty and then eat something too hot and end up drinking out of a vase. The rogues' gallery before him seemed to be attired in garments raided from the dead. As he regarded them, he bade a fond farewell to the flickering wraith of his reputation.

'Despite everything,' he announced, 'I shall now read what I can only describe as the last will and testament of Maggot Stone.' He shot a glance of distaste at the assembly and began.

'I guess I kicked the can and can't tell you how relieved I am to have found safe haven in the devil's abyss, where I can at least be assured of conversation conducted boldly and clearly, and where events occur according to reliably consistent principles. The disappointment and mayhem I suffered at your hands has been thrown into stark relief by this trivial inferno.

'Billy Panacea, mutant nephew — you are perched harpy-like on the brink of oblivion. I've known it since the christening, when your shades fell into the font. I have followed your subsequent career with horror and disquiet, not to mention a certain grandeur. You live your life like a waiter in a windtunnel. I wish I could punch the scales from your eyes. A fat lot of good this uncoordinated marauding will do when you no longer have your poor, querulous Ma to bust you out of the slammer.

'Brute Parker. Are there any sadder words in the English language? Propping up the gun cupboard, your barely articulate crowing makes you as pleasant for company as a jerrybuilt barrage balloon. In the entire course of your thirty-eight years you have never used a verb. You joined this species by the seat of your pants. I advise you to administer a bullet to your straining head. There's not a moment to lose.

'Mr Specter, you and I were never on friendly terms, and no wonder. I have lost count of those who have stood accused in the perjury room, hoping for representation of the exceptional calibre required when one is truly blameless, only to be confronted with you, a man medically certified as a quadruped. Your corroded wits are responsible for almost twenty-three percent of the misery in this state. At any given moment the killing jar is full to bursting with your clients, their faces flattened and distorted against the glass. For all they know you could be a penniless Sicilian organ-grinder. If you had a speck of honesty you'd flick it off your sleeve.

'Bleach Pastiche, your sanity is damaged below the waterline. You conduct your affairs with a comprehensive insolence and an almost chef-like disregard for morals and human life. The same goes for that clown who follows you around like an atomic shadow. The attraction is clearly pathological. You are nothing short of a berserk, exterminating bitch.

'Gilbert Wham, you first came to my attention when you upset a gong in the Shonen Restaurant on Chain Street. I forgot about you immediately, until just now. You're bone idle, and more than anything resemble a chemically-altered herring.

' I have less charity for you, Mr Toto. I confronted a burger at the Reaction Bar and felt as sick as a stoat. The regulars watched me as though awaiting an explosion. For days I suffered a malady which the experts could not identify, after which I returned to the bar to give you a damn good thrashing. Yet looking about me I perceived many less fortunate than myself — one was biting down on something which had the appearance and consistency of a poolside flotation toy, and another was screaming as though possessed. These are your people. In the journey from childhood to adolescence and back again, any principles you once held dear have dissolved like a tylenol. Your ghastly career is fuelled by macabre refreshments and deviant medicine, openly swallowed through a lab funnel. You are at your quietest when thinking aloud. I have it on good authority that your very existence is flatly illegal.'

Here she digressed briefly, cursing church and state, claiming a role in some minor shootings, pledging honour to the Reich and so on. Returning to the matter, Pert read on.

'Let's speak plainly — you are bastards to a man. This town is glassy-eyed with your felonies. You shore up your vacuity with a cop-baiting, dead-end-kid bravado. Your loyalties are misplaced and exclusive, and there is no telling where you will strike next. I have loathed your tusken features ever since you burst screaming through the fabric of our society, and now, as my remains sink below room temperature, I detest you all the more.'

Here the crescendo of allegations roof-rolled to a stop.

The Beretta crew, who thus far had gazed on as though preserved in borax, began to shift uncertainly. Glances collided and ricocheted at speed. Billy spectated the ceiling.

Finally, Parker broke the silence.

'When you're right, you're right,' he muttered, raising his eyebrows.

Before anyone could reply, the attorney turned a page.

'And as for the bequest,' he stated: 'You'll pretend with translucent predictability that your presence here is entirely altruistic, but I'll have you know as well as I do you'd turn up naked and draped in a python if there were smackers at stake. And there are. My entire fortune I bequeath to whichever one of you boggle-eyed aberrations manages to stay alive and kicking for precisely one week. That is all.'

It was like feeding a percussion cap to a ruminant. Voices and guns were simultaneously raised in an obliterative frenzy which tore the office to pieces. Even the mildest among them began to shriek like some bearded, blaspheming castaway. Mr Pert looked on with an expression as withering as the tree of life as the assembled louts embarked on a murderous bonanza, each spending ammo in inverse proportion to his intelligence.

They piled into the street baying like firehouse dogs, and over subsequent days the town bristled with sniper activity. Beetling along roof-edges, the potential beneficiaries tendered a volley of rounds for one another's consideration. Ventilation was not only desired but seemed economically unavoidable.

Yet ballistic dexterity was not enough when they began hiding out in the sewers, and after a week everyone was still in bounding health despite the best efforts of their friends and associates.

It took this long for the truth to crash home — they had been firing in the wrong direction.

Pooling their perceptions, all six agreed that the will they had heard was not the one they were familiar with. Pert must have rumbled everything immediately — even a cursory glance at the original would have revealed a mosaic of deceit and corruption. Billy had been the first to spin-dry the safe and alter the will. He had described himself therein as strenuously pious despite every circumstance and the one worthy heir. Billy had also boosted the cash from Maggot's account so as to be recompensed twice and excised the reference to his mother. Gilbert Wham had rolled and sold Maggot's vintage auto and inherited the insurance and fortune in his draft of the bequest. Billy had re-stolen the auto but in Bleach's draft Aunt Maggot claimed ownership of all Billy's property and bequeathed it to Bleach as well as implicating Parker in three homicides for which Bleach was responsible. The amendment leaving everything to Parker was written in yellow crayon and included references to a cache of ammo-guzzlers allegedly buried on the Maggot estate. Don Toto had busted in with Billy's old gang and amended Maggot's remarks in regard to his establishment, saying she 'loved the burger'. He'd get it all plus her posthumous nomination for his election to Mayor. This Harpoon amended to 'bricklayer', and as well as arranging his own affluent inheritance he attached a rider laying out in finely-crafted detail a scam to embezzle eight million smackers from the federal mint, which sum was to fund the construction of a monument to his sexual prowess. In addition to this he required a trouble-free seat in the House of Representatives and round-the-clock access to his drug of choice. As a legalistic afterthought he amended 'burger' to 'rat'.

Throughout the reading it had dawned on various parties that their amendments had not gone through. In reality they had rendered the will as void as a scooped land-crab and, seeing his opportunity, Pert had leapt at it with speed-stretched features. His reading of an unamended copy was intended to buy time — he knew they'd go at eachother like scorpions in a bottle, the conflict fanned by the assumption that one among them had switched the wills at the eleventh hour.

The crew bolted to Pert's office but the bastard had flown. The janitor said he'd seen him go off in a limo, shouting with laughter. Said it was great to see a guy enjoying his retirement. He'd be decanting into the Congo Basin by now and they could hardly bleat to the cops. While Specter viewed the scam with frank admiration, the others felt a writhing convolution of fury and respect. The brainer was that they'd followed Maggot's difficult instructions even as the fortune was leaving the country.

Behind locked doors at the Delayed Reaction, the group downed a vat of highgrade and considered their position. As night crept past and daylight trickled in like medication, all became horribly clear. Maggot had them bang to rights — they were the biggest morons this side of the fossil gap.

ROPE AND RICTUS

Ben Rictus was Elliot Rope's best and only fan. Rope was an author whose books were almost zoological in their shameless endorsement of happiness and laughter. He was forever writing about frenzied piano tuners, belligerent master chefs and people who were no longer responsible for their actions. He'd create the most floridly psychotic entanglement and then unravel it and watch the fireworks. Bizarre and constructive, he was like Kafka for grown-ups. Ben got a hell of a charge out of Rope's work and this was a guy who was so demanding of a book that he'd turn the pages by lashing them with a whip.

Ben only wished that everyone could appreciate Rope as he did. He'd compiled the collected works of Elly Rope despite the fact that Elly Rope was an author whose works were generally collected in the form of garbage. Rope's books had been printed on the cheap by Rope himself, and even now the denizens of Beerlight spoke of him as a rabid pamphleteer. It was said he'd sit in the Delayed Reaction Bar screaming about postmodernism. 'They say a dead man tells no tales,' he'd shout, 'but they've overlooked Martin Amis!' Rope once hacked his way into Don DeLillo's home computer and altered his latest novel so that one of the characters smiled. Later he created a tri-head virus which ran amok among the manuscript files at Random House rewriting them all grammatically. Growing bitter with non-publication, he became obsessed with the theory that publishers never look beyond the first page of unsolicited manuscripts, and to test it he submitted a novel of which only the first page was written sensibly, the rest consisting of the letter 'X' repeated one million seven hundred and thirty-one times. To his shock and embarrassment they agreed to publish the work. It was the final straw. Elly Rope set fire to the publishing house one turbulent night, destroying it and the manuscript. Then he disappeared like a shot and hadn't been seen for years. Ben Rictus never met him but since his discovery of Rope's first novel, *Punching Volunteers*, he had become a lone crusader for Rope's status as a literary barnstormer. He wanted to bring him out of hiding and make the world understand.

Now Ben Rictus was a storyteller in his own right and had trouble being legitimately published for the same two reasons as Elly Rope. First, the material was conspicuous — this is exactly what publishers are afraid of. A book should blend in to the point where in a tight spot they can claim it was never published atall.

Second was the unspoken belief that the expression of originality drained a limited pool of ideas — while Ben knew from experience that ideas are self-replenishing, like snot. Ben took the snail by the tail with a strategy to give both him and Elly Rope a shot at the bigtime. He'd take one of Elly Rope's better works — *Lord Pin Collapses*, say — and retype it as a manuscript. Then he'd submit it under his own name, hopefully get it through and enjoy (for a while at least) the raptures of authorship. Rope would drop everything and show up, indignantly claiming copyright in the work, at which distorted moment Ben would freely hand him the recognition he deserved. Ben didn't have a qualm as he figured plagiarism was just taking an author at his word, and anyway it was surely the kind of scorching subterfuge that Rope himself would endorse.

Well the first people who saw it bit the book out of Ben's unholy hand. Ben retitled it *Bellying Out Unexpectedly*, to delay Elly Rope's boneshattering rage until after publication, and six months later he was holding a copy: *Bellying Out Unexpectedly* by Ben Rictus — he'd pulled it off easier than a rubber mask.

As the novel climbed the bestseller list Ben lived in perpetual fear of being abruptly and irreversibly knifed by the wronged author. But Rope didn't show. He didn't even call. Ben was being hailed as a literary demigod, with a thirty thousand smacker advance for a second novel and talk-show invitations he could spit and hit — and Rope never came forward. Maybe he was someplace they don't have television — like

Canada. Maybe he'd been arrested for going mad and was sat rocking in the corner of a cell, eyes fixed and dilated. Maybe the guy was dead as a donut, leaving Ben to live a complete life in the bacchanalian style to which he was becoming accustomed.

Ben figured what the hell and let things slide. The second book he gave the publisher was one of his own — *My Crunchy Past* — and to his surprise this was more popular than the one Rope had written. The critics said by god he's coming on in bounds. They called him a frenzied individualist, and for the first time he believed them. After all, the latest book was totally on the level and it sold like underwear. Ben bought a yardpool as big as Pluto's moon and was as happy as a dog in a sidecar.

It was at this point that Elly Rope made his existence not unknown to the literary establishment, referring to Ben as the devil in human mould. He exploded onto national television stating that Ben was a death-dealing matriarch who if given a hammer would use it to smash the bill of a wren. Rope had simply been choosing his moment — now he claimed authorship not only of his own novel but of Ben's book into the bargain. The law believed him and Ben was impoverished, avoiding a prison term only by absconding to a republic the constitution of which was scrawled in crayon. Yet throughout the ordeal Ben felt a strange sense of acceptance and rare justice.

Meanwhile back home the public and publishers were for once in agreement — they wanted fresh material from Elly Rope. And Elly Rope had to admit privately that he was as dry as a bone — in fact he was spitting feathers. He hadn't an idea in his head, except to find Ben Rictus and strike a secret deal for new material. Ben's *Crunchy* novel was the most popular of Elly's books and there was an angry demand for more.

Elly Rope hired more private detectives than should ever have been born and when they found Ben Rictus they didn't tell Elly Rope for over a year. By the time Elly Rope confronted Ben Rictus on a small tropical jetty, Ben had gone native and was reeling in a sailfish the size of a buffalo. Ben had forgotten that Elly Rope existed. Life truly imitates art and since Ben was a plagiarist he found he fitted right in. He sent Elly away empty-handed save for his blessings and laughter.

Totally thrown, Elly went home and set about his new novel with all the inspiration of a dead cigarette. The novel was as dusty and hollow as a dried saint. It stormed the bestseller list and won three respected awards. As the most prestigious of these was pressed into his quiescent hand, the author was weeping. Once again, Elly Rope had been shafted.

STACKED

Jerry Diesel was a preventive escape artist — he never got locked up. He also had more connections than a plate of spaghetti, and when at the age of thirty-five he decided to retire he enlisted the aid of the entire Beerlight underworld in a final collaborative bank haul.

The job was planned in fly-leg detail. Jerry would check a bomb into a safe deposit box at the McKenna Square bank — he had stored explosives there before but on this occasion they were set to go off in the dead of night and pour smoke into the square. A slabhead unit would give the fire department the cod-eye and drive a couple of trucks to the scene in full garb, making a ruckus and collecting the cash. Cop impersonators would stand around yelling and pacify onlookers by shooting them. It would be the biggest knockover in the annals of post-latest-war America.

Nearly everybody was there, among them Freddy Bitmap, Backhaul Fairlight, Sam Transam, Tim Canada, John Rag-Hip, Jerry Earl, Mercy Goat, Gilbert Wham, Audrey Benelin, Babyface Terrier, Dino Harmaline, Ignore Henry, Sam 'Sam' Bleaker, Doll-Gone-Wrong, Barry Ultimatum, Leone Vanguard, Jammy Le Mot, John 'Kickstart' Kelly, Harry Hydrocele, Fourth of July Skeleton, Hugo Peppercorn, Chewy Endeavour, Ferris Malady, Hammy Roadstud, Ban Saliva, Brenda Divorce and Terry 'It's Raining Snow' McFadden.

Billy Distend took off his hat as a disguise. Ike 'Knuckles' Naysayer was head of the IC mob — he was called Knuckles because that was as far as he ever got into a bank vault before getting arrested. Head of the slabheads was Holder Fray, a notorious drunkard and truck-roller. After overseeing the abstraction of the blaze department he drove the head truck with a blathering indolence which ruptured the credulity of those aboard. Holder had a convulsing arm and a false eye, regrettably made of corduroy, and the truck ploughed through the cop impersonators, squealing like a banana skin on a bonfire. It plunged without restraint into the front of the bank and, stumbling amid the rubble of his derelict morality, Holder was stabbed enthusiastically by his colleagues. The bank was burning like an effigy.

The real cops arrived at the broiling devastation and were welcomed with open arms fire. Henry Blince shouted through a megaphone that the horde should throw down their weapons and save their comments for later. This provoked a volley of mind-boggling obscenities and ferocious flak which shredded the cop barricades and forced the cops to fire back encouragingly. The battle developed into a classic pattern of maudlin codependence. Knuckles Naysayer was shot seven times in the belly and hadn't the imagination to double over. Barry Ultimatum was smacked by a cop shell-launcher, getting a scorch-hole in his shirt which would subsequently remind the coroner of the US flag. Gilbert Wham was shot, to his lasting advantage. The slabheads were mistaking the depleted IC mob for real cops and shooting them down. Some were shot from both directions, among them young Backhaul Fairlight, whose assassination of Viscount Strange had been described by the cognoscenti as 'promising'. Ballistic talent expired by the busload. The slabhead crew fired tearfully from behind the two burning fire trucks. Some got away. The money burnt. It was a heroic shambles deserving of a freeze-frame. But Jerry Diesel never saw it because he wasn't there. He was at the other end of town single-handedly robbing a bank on Curve Street. The alarm tripped but the cops at McKenna Square figured it was just a decoy.

STRESSWORLD

Harpoon Specter was all fired up with the notion of a theme park in honour of Beerlight. Stressworld was to be the last word in artificial mayhem, an automated environment of paranoia and hostility from which the paying public would fight tooth and nail to escape, sustaining injury and profound mental trauma. Specter saw it as an authentic urban experience, air-conditioned by the sighs of the suicidal. Drive-by killings would occur on the half-hour. Visitors would run screaming from berserk automatons. Dismal conversations would take place. Satisfaction would be a rumour.

Grabbing the nettle, he hired the animatronics engineer Sparky Tafero. Tafero had been kicked out of Disneyland when he rewired Abe Lincoln to blather accusations of barnyard bestiality to the assembled vacationers, and he now allowed himself to be convinced that Stressworld was the next step in his disastrous career. Specter kissed his money goodbye and sank it into the project. As a showpiece to woo potential backers he commissioned a costive replica of the Delayed Reaction Bar on a lot near the Loop Expressway. The interior was reproduced down to the crest pattern on the smallest adder. The fact that most of the Reaction regulars are bone idle was a boon to Sparky, who populated the bar with an assortment of boss-eyed dummies which never moved a muscle. If these rock-hard mannequins were addressed or approached, they were programmed simply to explode. This was the easiest way to camouflage their lack of sophistication. Behind the bar was a fully mechanised imitation of Don Toto, and in the corner stood a sentimental copy of Auto-Rhino, rigged to club anyone who stepped within twelve yards. Henry Blince — who in reality rarely visited the Delayed Reaction — was represented by a kind of balloon. This was inflated and deflated rapidly by means of a concealed hydraulic hose-bundle, so that he appeared to be panting heavily. It took months to synchronise the baring of Parker's teeth with the extending of his knife arm, but when Sparky got it running he and Harpoon knew they were on the up and up. It was time to invite the investors.

Back in town, Specter had related his concept in only the broadest terms. He wanted them to sample the experience for themselves, and so one stark evening three men of finance drove up to the complex which housed the Reaction environment. At the end of a vaulted corridor, they entered a dim chamber and stood, briefcases in hand. They seemed to be in some kind of subterranean bistro. As their eyes adjusted to the gloom, they perceived a number of inert dummies, painted up as though to ward off evil spirits. Some were tipped aside like the quietly deceased. The place was as still as a storeroom.

They advanced into the room, apprehensive and afraid. Then the foremost spotted a fat guy sat at a table, breathing heavily, lolling, staring into space. As he approached the figure, a jukebox sparked into life, illuminating the barman's death-head grin. Some of the dummies began to move. One of the investors became manly and bluff, and perched at the bar. The barman smiled over his head, wiping one glass.

Another placed his case on a table and sat opposite Henry Blince.

'So,' he said, nervously amicable. 'What's the deal?'

The fat man heaved a deep breath, his head falling back, and then began to hyperventilate alarmingly. The investor's heart beat like a mill as he watched the figure convulse, its head tossing at violent speed. It proceeded to emit a high-pitched squeal like a punctured bathtoy. The financier signalled uncertainly to his colleague at the bar, who was too busy ordering a beer.

The barman had begun to shudder, and now let out a congested shriek and punched the banker in the forehead. As the guy lay identifying the Plough, Toto bellowed a loop of prerecorded profanities and threw his fists at empty air. Foam streamed from the dead mouth of a patron seated bolt-upright on a barstool.

The potential backers watched with an unnamed horror.

The third man, who until now had been paralysed with fear, lunged forward to retrieve his felled colleague, yelling at the other to run for his life. Overstepping the mark, he detonated two regulars and fired Auto from the corner like a cork from a bottle — the primitive effigy collided with a table and blew deafeningly to pieces. Brute Parker levitated through a trapdoor, halting with a thump. 'Name one permanent structure,' it said, then bared its teeth, raised a Kalashnikov and swept a 180-degree arc. Beerbottles exploded and the gibbering Toto was punctured repeatedly across the chest. The jukebox was playing backwards. Lights began to gutter and short. The motionless barfly was frothing like an oil-gush and the visitors waded kneedeep in industrial foam, screaming like the damned. Parker's dummy turned back and forth, firing on full-auto. The air furnaced with destruction and cordite fumes, like a poltergeist on parole. Ducking a hail of shrapnel, the financiers hit the door running. Behind them, the dummies were jangling like a can-string alarm.

In a media van parked nearby, Specter and Tafero watched the pixilated, silent monitor image of their guests' screaming faces and knew they were in business. Flushed with laughter and exchanging hearty congratulations, they proceeded lustily to the complex exit. The money men burst out on a wave of gunsmoke, babbling and swiping at imaginary fiends. One had become white-haired with terror and another fell to his knees and ate sand. The third would not stop screaming, his face ravaged and demented.

Beaming with success, Specter and Tafero stepped up with a contract and a fountain pen. 'I think we understand eachother,' Specter told them with a suave smirk, and found his hairstyle abruptly rearranged by skid-wind from the departing cars. He looked down at the contract, which appeared to have been savagely mauled by some ferocious animal. He watched his backing head for the hills. Interweaving dust-tracks glowed in the twilight like the trail of snails. So much for innovation. What did they want — fantasy?

Meanwhile the investors were feeling as wrecked and relieved as the survivor in a slasher movie. Everything was raw and immediate. They pulled over in town, thirsting for normality. Shambling down the sidewalk, they argued about their next move. They had to get some perspective, sit down and pan it out — they had to get a few drinks inside them. Supporting eachother, they pushed open a door and entered the Delayed Reaction Bar.

FALL OUT

One night while having a nightmare I found that I was being chased by the wrong monster. I was scrabbling up a steep embankment when I happened to glance back and realised I'd never seen this thing before. It obviously saw me at the same moment, as it stopped shrieking and lowered its claws, squinting at me. Well, after our initial embarrassment we got to talking at a nearby saloon, which was full of inverted staircases and vats of dough.

'I am most surprised to see you in the tangled forest tonight,' said the creature, who told me his name was Ramone. 'I am usually charged with the duty of chasing Brute Parker who owns the all-night gun shop on the corner of Dive and Ride. He is a most desperate character. He weeps aloud when I chase him, and begs for mercy. And what's more, he wears pink and yellow pyjamas, and it is not a pretty sight.'

At this point I needed the bathroom and asked the

monster to excuse me, but afterwards, this being a dream, I couldn't for the life of me find my way back to the bar.

Bright and early the next morning I don't know what I was thinking — maybe I was still half-asleep — but without consulting Bleach or the Bible I went over to Parker's all-night gun shop to brag of my knowledge. 'Parker,' I said, entering grandly, 'you're a mockery and a sham.'

Parker looked up from a back issue of *Throat-Knife*, taking in the information I had imparted. 'What did you just say?' he rumbled, frowning. Parker frowned differently from other people because, he said, he kept his forehead at a lower temperature.

'I said you're a sobbing sham and yes a fraud — pretending to be a bastard. Ramone has told me all about it.'

'Ramone. Who the fuck is Ramone?'

'The freak who interrupts your sleep every night,' I announced with breezy confidence. 'The monster who pursues you through the forest even as you wear pink and yellow pyjamas, you hypocrite.'

'What?'

'Begging for mercy. Weeping to beat the band. And I bet you dreamt of a totally new mutant last night — am I right you faker?'

Parker folded his magazine neatly and placed it aside. He stood and walked slowly around the counter, placed his hands on either side of my head and began with all his strength to exert pressure inward. He began to shudder and flush red as I had seen Rutger

Hauer do while crushing someone's head in *Blade Runner* — I found myself wondering why this was, and whether the look could be reproduced without the effort and expense of crushing a head. The whole scene fuzzed into black and white, and I was next aware of Parker speaking to me. He had placed my head in the store vice and was slowly winding the handle. 'Do you want to know what I really dreamt about last night, clown?' All I could see was the vice-metal and table edge as Brute related his dream. In the dream he stumbled through the jeering alleys of Jerusalem under the weight of a GE antipersonnel bazooka which he carried like a yoke. All the Delayed Reaction regulars were there throwing stones and beercans. Even Brute could perceive the symbolic parallels and was filled with the Christlike dread of becoming an institution unrelated to his beliefs. He would rather have died, but knew this wouldn't make any difference. Beginning to rage, he struggled at the ropes which bound him to the GE gun. He got one hand free enough to squeeze the trigger, blowing a hole in the crowd to his left. His laughter merged with the screams of onlookers as he wheeled about and fired indiscriminately into them. The dream ended here because, Brute explained, dreams always end before you kill the last person.

I gasped something about it being a sex thing. I could feel my skull beginning to splinter and at this most crucial of moments a customer chugged into the gun shop. As Brute went to serve him I fumbled for the handle and loosened the grip enough to release my head and stagger upright. I had a poison headache, but at least it was portable; I stumbled groaning through the store, knocking everything over in a blind bid for the cops. Citizens with a downer on the cops are always the first to run to them when danger erupts — especially in places where citizens are not allowed by law to own firearms for personal protection. Elsewhere they are numbered among the erupters. Running, I thanked my lucky stars I was only the victim.

Before I could change my mind I was in a back room at the cop den, tied to a chair. A cop regarded me, his face a mask of disapproval. He said he didn't like my kind and I was filled with the delirious expectation that he would identify me as a common species — that there were others like myself. I controlled my excitement, but he seemed to sense it — his gaze wavered uncertainly.

Before either of us could speak a door opened and Chief of the Cops Henry Blince entered with difficulty. 'This the clown, Benny?' he said, gesturing at me with a cigar, and I plaintively explained what had happened at Parker's. The part about Ramone made them shout with incredulous laughter. Bleach had told me that reality was fiction in another shape and I told them this, but it only made them laugh all the more. Benny was having to turn round and kick at the wall, and Blince cried. At least I was making an impression. Then they sniggered something about provocation. Growing indignant, I related Bleach's theory that there is a parallel universe containing a Beerlight in which the cops behave impeccably and that next to that is a third in which they are only human. Benny ran out abruptly with a hand to his mouth, having laughed so much he had coughed something up. Blince intercepted his tears with both fists and gasped at me to stop. He went outside to collect Benny, and after more distant, reverberating hilarity they re-entered, wiping their eyes.

'I like you, you goddamn astro-monkey,' Blince told me, chortling, and proceeded to relate how essential it was I assassinate Brute Parker in order to avoid arrest and imprisonment for whatever they could stand in the perjury room. They couldn't be involved and it was common knowledge me and Parker were at throat-punching odds. All the cops would do was carry out a legitimate blaze-raid on Parker's premises during a lunch break. Finding his store and home a scorched silhouette, Parker would storm unarmed toward the cop den, during which storming I would economise his breathing with an Uzi 9mm, right there in the street. Blince said it was time I repaid my debt to society.

They left me in an overnight cell with Parker's file. Tomorrow was the day. The file said that Brute had spent his early childhood among priests who taught him that it was necessary to suffer to obtain happiness, and wishing to bestow such happiness upon those same priests, Brute had tortured them beyond all recognition. Today no such goodwill existed in his heart. Mistaking it for a burglar, he had shot his guardian angel. Brute went about the dealing of cod-eyes with a rage which was commendable when compared with the desultory violence exhibited by the mob and cops. I once asked him why he was so unhappy and he looked into the horizon and said, 'Instinct.'

That night my nightmare was back to normal. Flagging him down and stopping everything, I asked my usual monster what had happened to Ramone. He lit a cigarette and said he'd never heard of the guy, but that last night he'd found himself in some place like Jerusalem. 'Look what I found there.' And he showed me a handful of sand and 7.62mm slugs.

The next day there's a grey funnel of smoke above the Beretta Triangle. I stand on Sunday Street with a cop Uzi semiauto under a black full-length, leaning against the wall. Parker marching calm up the street toward me. I stand away from the wall. Brute looking beyond me. I draw the semiautomatic. Brute doesn't flinch or slow, though he sees the gun. I hand it to him as he passes and continues on to the den. I walk home. Several controlled, emphatic shots ring out as I round up Bleach, load the car and drive.

I remember Chief Blince's remark about repaying my debt to society. I don't believe in revenge.